The Book of Lucifer
and Other New
Sherlock Holmes Stories

By

Alan Dimes

Edited by David Marcum

Paperback ISBN 978-1-80424-556-9
ePub ISBN 978-1-80424-557-6
PDF ISBN 978-1-80424-558-3

Published by MX Publishing
335 Princess Park Manor, Royal Drive,
London, N11 3GX
www.mxpublishing.com

Cover design by Awan

To the memory of my father James William Dimes (1921-2011) and of my mother, Doris Eva Dimes (1923-2013)

Contents

The Book of Lucifer   1

The Conk-Singleton Forgery   28

The Adventure of the Elfrincham Maze   50

The Taverne Emerald   79

Dinner at St. Luke's   105

The Adventure of James Edward Phillimore   119

The Adventure of the Unfortunate Cardinal   144

The Disappearance of the Cutter *Alicia*   161

The Book of Lucifer

My readers may remember the sensational trial of The Legion of Lucifer, some years ago, which resulted in the execution of the leader and several members of that repellant organization. It may also be recalled that the judge praised the efforts of those Scotland Yard officials who had been instrumental in bringing the culprits to justice. What went unsaid, as is so frequently the case, was the aid given them by my friend and colleague, Mr. Sherlock Holmes. It is true that the matter did not afford him much opportunity to exercise his outstanding powers of logic and deduction, but it is equally true that, without his knowledge and insight, the official force would have had little to work with. On this basis, and considering the intrinsic interest of the case, I have decided, with Holmes's consent, to lay the full story of his involvement before the reading public.

During his three-year absence from London, there had been, as he pointed out to Inspector Lestrade upon his return in 1894, three unsolved murders.

"Perhaps you'd like to take a look at them, Mr. Holmes," the inspector remarked when he called on us one evening a few days later, "and see if you can make anything of them."

Holmes agreed, with the proviso that he would naturally give priority to any current case of interest or importance on which he was consulted. He was given access to the Scotland Yard files, from which I am not permitted to quote, but after Holmes's supposed death I had maintained a keen interest in crime and kept a scrapbook of newspaper clippings concerning those I considered of most importance. I draw on these to provide a brief outline of each case as it was seen by the public.

John Cooper Whitney was regarded by all who knew him as an upstanding member of society. A lifelong Liberal and a personal friend of Lord Bellinger, he was also a member of the Methodist Church and an early and active supporter of the National Temperance Foundation. His large personal fortune came from his ownership of several cotton mills in the north of England, where his teetotal principles were strictly adhered to – any worker who was found drinking at work was summarily dismissed, and any worker who brought alcohol onto the premises was fined, and suspended from work for a period of two weeks. Any worker who was found guilty of offences involving alcohol outside the factory gates was also subject to dismissal, even though he had already been fined by the authorities.

Whitney had a large house in Rochdale, but spent most of his time at his spacious flat in Victoria Street, which he preferred for its proximity to the Houses of Parliament. He was unmarried and lived alone. He had three servants, a cook, butler, and maid who did not live in, but were employed under the same conditions as his mill hands, and liable to be out of their situation if they were caught drinking or in possession of alcohol. On the morning of April 27th, 1893, his current servants arrived at the flat to find their employer lying dead on the carpet of his living room, clad only in his nightshirt. His throat had been cut. The servants immediately went out into the street to find a constable, and within an hour two detectives and the coroner were present. There were no signs of a forced entry.

The murder was, of course, reported in the newspapers, and while he was well known within his own circles, there can be no doubt that, in the south of England at least, he became better known in death than he had been in life. As his life came under public scrutiny, it became clear that opinion on John Cooper Whitney was sharply divided. For every person who had come to the conclusion that he was a man of steely principle who had worked hard to rescue the labouring classes from the evils of drink, there was another who thought he was a damned interfering busybody who had no right to attempt to deprive the workers of one of the few pleasures they could afford. But could someone who held the latter view have hated him enough, or thought him enough of a threat to personal freedom, to have somehow entered – or been let into – his house to kill him?

With the assistance of the Lancashire police, Scotland Yard attempted to draw up a list of everyone who might have had a grudge against Whitney. I use the word "attempted" because he had been in charge of the family mills for forty-five years, and the number of people who had been fired because of his draconian attitudes ran into the hundreds. He had owned the flat in Westminster for twenty years, and in that time he had dismissed four cooks, three maids, and five butlers for alcoholic offences.

The two police forces visited as many people on their list as they could, but found no one who didn't have an alibi, or was dead or had left the country. The three servants, and especially the butler, Lawson, fell under suspicion. The butler because he, other than Whitney himself, alone had a key to the flat, so he could have arrived earlier than usual and surprised his master in bed. Both cook and maid testified that he had in fact arrived last that morning, and that they had had to wait to be let in. Perhaps all three had conspired to kill him?

Witnesses came forward who had seen all the servants riding on the bus or underground after the time which the coroner determined to be that of Whitney's death. The suggestion was made in one of the more sensational newspapers that he had been done away with by someone hired by a cabal of disgruntled brewers whose livelihood he threatened.

"Despite the high profile of the National Temperance Foundation," said Holmes as we discussed the case one afternoon, *"it is doubtful that their influence, and especially that of one member, would be strong enough to spread fear amongst the brewers and distillers, nor that they would have resorted to murder had it been so. There are adherents of temperance in Parliament who would surely have been a more important target for an alcohol advocating assassin. You realize, of course, Watson, that despite the evidence of the other servants, and those who saw him on public transport, the butler is not exonerated."*

"Why do you say so?"

"He held one of the two keys, and keys can be copied. While it seems unlikely that he struck the blow himself, he may have facilitated the entry of the person who did. I shall recommend to Lestrade that he question Lawson further."

During the summer months, it was common for Martin Eastwick and his wife Joan to cross the small stretch of Hampstead Heath that separated their house in Spaniards Road from the Vale of Health, where Mrs. Eastwick's parents, Michael and Susannah Pope, lived, and, after their visit, return home by the same route. On June 22nd, 1893, Mrs. Eastwick made the short journey on her own as her husband was away on a business trip. According to Mr. and Mrs. Pope, their daughter stayed rather later than usual. She refused their offer of her old room and set off for her home in the dark.

An elderly gentleman who was out on his morning constitutional found her body at seven a.m. the next day. She had been strangled. As her rings, necklace, earrings, and purse were missing, the police concluded that robbery had been the motive. The value of the jewellery and money amounted to about forty-five pounds, a sum for which someone living rough on the heath (of whom there were several) might be prepared to kill. All the tramps known to be sleeping on the heath were rounded up and subjected to intense interrogation, but none confessed.

"Really, Watson, if you were homeless and sleeping on the heath, would you stay there after you had killed a woman and stolen forty-five pounds?"

"What should Lestrade have done, then?"

"He should have asked all the other tramps on the heath if one of their number was missing, and if so, whether they knew his name."

"Such people tend not to stay in one place for long," I said, "so it's unlikely that they are still all there to question."

"True. But then he should have gone to all the hotels and boarding houses in the immediate vicinity to see if any had rented a room to a obvious tramp with the unexpected ability to pay for it. That avenue of enquiry still remains."

"Supposing someone had another motive for killing the woman, and a tramp merely found her and took the money from her dead body?"

"That is a definite possibility, yet you will agree that in either case, a tramp must at least be looked for. Another possibility of course is that, as you say, someone had a motive other than theft, but took the money and jewelry to make it seem the work of a thief. There are certainly difficulties there. Mr. and Mrs. Eastwick, and Mrs. Eastwick's parents, all appear to be upstanding citizens with no enemies in the world."

Since the death of his only child, his son David, Abraham Weston, a widower, had become increasingly reclusive, until he took this tendency to an extreme, selling his house in Camberwell and moving to a lonely little cottage on a remote promontory on the west coast of Scotland. His only human contact was with a middle-aged lady, Mrs. Laurie, who cycled to his home from the nearest village once a week, bringing him groceries and staying to clean the cottage. Every other week she took his laundry and returned it the following week. She testified that while he paid her generously for these services, he spoke to her very little during her visits, preferring either to closet himself in his study with his books or go for a walk across the windswept terrain while she attended to the housework.

She arrived at about half-past-ten on the morning of July 24th that same year and found Weston in his study, dead from a single gunshot wound to the head. A sturdy, sensible woman, Mrs. Laurie didn't succumb to hysteria, but immediately jumped on her bicycle and pedalled swiftly home and reported the death to the village constable, who then sent a message to the authorities in Ullapool. From there, the responsibility for investigation was handed over to the police in Edinburgh, and then to the Scotland Yarders, who in truth stood little better chance of finding the culprit. They questioned the folk in the village to see if any strangers had been seen in the area at the time, but none had. No one amongst the villagers had any motive, and indeed, the only item in the cottage of any obvious value, a silver teapot, hadn't been removed. The detectives then switched their inquiries to Camberwell, where their efforts proved equally fruitless.

"The fact that no one in the village saw any strangers hardly proves anything," said Holmes. "According to the medical report, the murder must have taken place in the hours of darkness. When we combine this with the fact that Weston's house was on a promontory, we can at least surmise that the killer arrived at night in a boat, committed the deed, then left by the way he came."

Holmes looked at the cases from time to time when the steady stream of new clients which attended his return to active practice permitted, but in the end was forced to confess that while he could get a little further than the official force, he was still unable to produce anything conclusive.

The situation would have remained thus, had it not been for the occurrence of five more murders which were equally baffling and seemingly insoluble . . . .

"Ali Ben Abou" was the stage name of Norman Waters, the forty-two-year-old son of a lighterman from Bermondsey, who had been an entertainer in the music halls, in various capacities, after starting as a stagehand at the age of fifteen. By the time he was twenty-nine, he had established himself as a magician.

At the climax of his act, a marked bullet appeared to be placed in a gun and fired at Ali, who seemed to catch it in his teeth. A member of the audience was called up on stage to mark the bullet, fire the gun, and identify the bullet when the magician removed it from his mouth. Despite the loud report and the large puff of smoke, it was of course a blank that was fired. The conjuror palmed the marked bullet, held his hand up to his teeth and produced it as if he had caught it in them. On this occasion, however, the young woman Ali called to assist him was horrified when she fired the gun and he fell forward with a cry, shot through the heart. As the blood spread across the front of his silken tunic, his unwitting killer fainted. The audience sat in stunned silence for a few moments. Then there was uproar.

The curtain was dropped, and a minute or two later the manager came from behind it to assure the crowd that an ambulance had been called, and under the circumstances could the auditorium please be cleared.

Waters' dressing room was locked, and when the police arrived they insisted that it be unlocked. The master key was obtained from the theatre's doorkeeper and entry effected. There, on the dressing table, they found an open box of blanks, or at any rate, a box proclaiming itself to be such. In fact, it contained real live bullets. The murderer must have emptied the box and made the substitution.

Waters was a notorious womaniser, and had been married three times, on all three occasions to women working in his act, which he had been doing for thirteen years. Such was his easy charm that his two previous wives seemed to have accepted their situation with equanimity and bore him no malice, as far as one could tell. Indeed, one of them had carried on acting as one of his assistants even after she had been replaced in his affections. There was always a possibility that a jealous husband or fiancé or a slighted lover had killed him, and the police investigated that line thoroughly.

The obvious suspect, the only conspicuous enemy that Waters had, was another magician, "Mehemet the Magnificent", (born Alfred Leaman in Stockwell, 1853) who had been loud in his claims that Waters had stolen some of his tricks, and had based the Middle Eastern flavour of his identity on Leaman's act. On the night that Waters was killed, Leaman was himself on the stage, in the middle of his own act at the Camden Palais. It was of course possible that he had hired someone to kill Waters. The police investigated this aspect and could find no evidence for it.

Waters' assistants, including his wife, were all questioned by the police, along with the magician's behind-the-scenes staff. The regular Empire stagehands could be ruled out because they weren't privy to the magician's secrets, and Ali was strict about keeping his dressing room door locked when he wasn't in it. A thorough investigation of Waters' employees revealed that none of them had anything against him. They had all been with him for years, and he was a fair and conscientious employer.

The doorkeeper was briefly suspected, as his master key gave him access to Waters' dressing room at all times, but he could account for all his movements on that last day of Waters' life and hadn't been out of anybody's sight long enough to effect the substitution. His wife confirmed that he had come home at the usual time the previous evening and had been at home the entire night.

Quentin Maltravers was in his seventieth year and had sat on the bench for twenty, after a successful career as a Q.C. During his time as a barrister he had specialized in prosecution, and so it came as little surprise that when he was elevated to the High Court, he quickly became noted for the severity of his judgements. In his personal life, he was a bachelor of ascetic tastes, whose principal vice appeared to be the occasional pinch of snuff. He belonged to only one club, the Solomon, whose membership was restricted to sitting and retired judges.

It came as a great surprise and shock, then, when this pillar of society was found beaten to death in one of the least salubrious back alleys in Whitechapel. Had he been a secret participant in the various forbidden pleasures afforded by London's East End? Whether that were true or not, there was no doubt that the number of people who had a motive for his murder ran into the hundreds.

When Lady Violet Cantwell, the youngest daughter of Lord Caithness, was presented at court, there had been general agreement that she was the most beautiful debutante of her season, and now, some fifteen years later, it couldn't be denied that maturity had only increased her charms. As well as her physical attractions, she had an open-hearted and forgiving nature, which won her friends of all religious and political persuasions.

In those days of her youth, there had been much competition for her hand. Eventually it seemed clear to all that John Allingham, a subaltern in the Household Cavalry and the only son and heir of Sir Walter Allingham, had won her heart, and that their marriage would soon be announced. There was much surprise, then, when she became the second wife of Lord Kilgarriff, a widower eighteen years her senior. In some quarters, there was speculation that she was marrying the wealthy aristocrat because Lord Caithness was deep in debt, and that she was sacrificing her own happiness to keep her parents from penury and disgrace.

Whatever the truth of the matter, it soon became obvious that the marriage was far from happy. After thirteen years, Lady Violet had failed to produce an heir, a fact which Kilgarriff continually threw in her face. He embarked on a series of liaisons with other women, and didn't attempt to conceal them from her.

John Allingham, now Sir John since the death of his father, had remained unmarried. Lady Violet at first sought him out as a friend, and a sympathetic ear for her troubles, but, inevitably, the passionate love which had once existed between them was rekindled. So deep was that love that it couldn't be hidden from society at large, and both Lady Violet and Sir John were prepared to face scandal and divorce if it meant that they could finally be together. Lord Kilgarriff refused to grant a divorce, and there the matter stood, until one morning the bodies of Sir John and Lady Violet were found floating in the Grand Union Canal.

Lord Kilgarriff was the most obvious suspect, but at the time their drowned corpses were discovered, he had been at his estate in the Scottish Highlands for ten days, in the company of a young local woman, and his staff could bear witness to the fact.

There was a suggestion that the lovers had had a mutual suicide pact due to the intractability of their situation, but friends of both denied that this could be so. The couple, they said, had been determined to live through the situation, come what might.

Giuseppe Parisi arrived in London from the seaport of Gioia Tauro in Calabria, in southern Italy, and went straight to that little triangle formed by Rosebery Avenue, Farringdon Road, and the Clerkenwell Road which is variously known as the Italian Quarter, Little Italy, or Italian Hill. Parisi had no marketable skills – at least, none that were legal, other than his great strength. He soon became known in the area as a man to go to when heavy lifting was needed, and this provided him with a reasonable income. He became engaged to one Theresa Prezzemoli, daughter of a local trader, and it must have seemed to him that he had an opportunity to lead an honest, safe, and productive life. Then, six months after his arrival, Theresa, worried that she hadn't seen her fiancé for three days, went to his landlady, Signora Barbieri, and asked her to unlock the door to Giuseppe's room. Inside, the two women were horrified to find him hanging upside down from a gas fitting on the ceiling, his body naked and his skin a ghastly white. His throat had been cut and he had been allowed to bleed to death like a slaughtered pig.

Theresa fell into uncontrollable hysteria. Signora Barbieri did her best to look after her and sent another of her lodgers, Franco Vitale, to fetch the police. It transpired that Franco and Guiseppe had become friends, and that one evening, after they had shared a bottle or two of wine, Giuseppe had told Franco the full story of his life – that he wasn't, as he told everybody, Guiseppe Parisi from Salerno, who had been a sailor all his life, but Guiseppe Baldini of Naples, bandit and assassin. He had sworn Vitale to secrecy, on pain of his life, but now, as Baldini could no longer harm him, nor be harmed by the disclosure, Vitale told the police all that he knew.

There was one thing about the crime that Vitale and all the Italian community knew, which was that hanging a man upside down after his death was a sign that he had been killed because he was a traitor. Had an avenger followed Baldini's trail, all the way from Calabria to Little Italy? It seemed the only solution, and yet extensive questioning of virtually everyone in the district yielded up no clues.

Like many young aristocrats of the time, the Honourable Harold Hamilton-Acott devoted most of his time to the pursuit of pleasure. He was a frequenter of the music hall and the racetrack, but was most often to be seen playing roulette at Porter's, his club in Pall Mall. Porter's facilities included bedrooms for those of its members who could not, or did not wish to travel home after a late night at the club. So great was Hamilton-Acott's devotion to the wheel that he sometimes spent an entire week there, remaining awake until three or four in the morning, repairing to an available bedroom and then emerging in time for a lavish meal before returning to the tables. According to fellow habitues, and the club's staff, he was merely a fair player, neither winning nor losing a great deal of money on most evenings. The family fortune was considerable, and the allowance supplied by his father, the sixth duke of Conway, was extremely generous, so he might have been a far worse player and still able to carry on with his obsession.

His lack of large wins meant that he made no enemies among his fellow players due to deprivation or envy. His erotic liaisons tended to be either paying encounters with high-class courtesans, or love affairs with unattached women of his own social circle who shared his easygoing attitude towards the whole business of *l'amour*. It was unlikely, therefore, that when he was fatally stabbed outside his rooms at the Albany, his murderer had been either another gambler or a jealous husband or fiancé. After several days at Porter's, Hamilton-Acott decided it was time to go home, because the next day was the Derby Stakes at Epsom and he wished to attend. He took a cab from Porter's at five in the morning and was found dead in the foyer about an hour later, with seven knife wounds in his back. None of the other occupants of the Albany heard anything suspicious.

Scotland Yard did not come to Sherlock Holmes with these matters. It was their belief that their usual methods – the application of more detectives to the case, and the extensive questioning of witnesses – would yield whatever solutions were possible.

Nevertheless, Holmes was deeply interested in them, and followed the progress of the investigations with avidity, returning to them whenever his current cases allowed. Then one morning as we sat reading the newspapers, he threw *The Daily Chronicle* down on the table with an exclamation of impatience.

"What is it?" I asked.

He made no reply, but reached over to his pipe rack and took out the cherry-wood. I remained silent, as I knew that this meant he was in a contentious mood. He stood and went over to the mantelpiece, where he filled the pipe from his Persian slipper, pressing tobacco into the bowl with his long thin fingers.

"Those murders are connected," he said, tossing his spent match into the grate.

"Which murders?"

"Why, man, the murders of Waters, Judge Maltravers, Giuseppe Baldini. Hamilton-Acott and Sir John Allingham and Lady Kilgarriff."

The notion seemed so absurd to me that although I had determined not to engage in conversation with him while he was in a disputatious frame of mind, I exclaimed, "Really, Holmes, how can they be? Waters was shot, Maltravers was beaten to death, Baldini's throat was cut, Hamilton-Acott was stabbed, and Sir John and Lady Violet were drowned. It isn't even sure if the last two really were murdered. Waters and Baldini came from a different social class. Surely all they have in common is that their killings are unsolved and, as far as I can see, likely to remain so."

"Nevertheless, I am convinced that there is a thread that binds them together."

"Until you can tell me what it is, you can hardly expect me to believe that. You have said yourself, there are unsolved crimes aplenty, and for all your powers, you are only one man."

"The knowledge is somewhere in my brain. I merely need to find it and bring it to bear. Will you give me your gift of silence for an hour or two?"

"Certainly. I'll do better than that: I shall go for a walk in the park."

When I returned at eleven o'clock, Holmes sprang from his armchair with a smile.

"You have found a connection then?"

"Yes, old friend. Does this mean anything to you?"

He handed me a piece of paper on which he had written:

John Cooper Whitney: Temperance
Joan Eastwick: The Female Pope
Abraham Weston: The Hermit
Norman Waters: The Magician
Quentin Maltravers: Judgement
Lady Kilgarriff and Sir John Allingham: The Lovers
Giuseppe Baldini: The Hanged Man
Harold Hamilton-Acott: The Wheel of Fortune

"The three previous murders are also part of this? I'm sorry, Holmes, but I am none the wiser. What does all this mean?"

"Have you heard of the Tarot?"

"Something to do with fortune telling, isn't it? Like tea leaves and palmistry. Stuff and nonsense. We are men of science, Holmes."

"Agreed, but as men of science, we must acknowledge the existence of other methods of thought and accept that there are those who follow them, no matter how unscientific they may seem to us. Such a system is the Tarot. You are correct in saying that it is often used as a device for fortune telling, but I suspect that our murderer thinks that he has found something more profound within it."

"Murderer? Singular? One man has perpetrated all these atrocities?"

"I think that one person is ultimately responsible for these crimes, though I don't doubt he has agents who do much of the work, the investigation . . . and sometimes the killing."

So saying, he reached into the pocket of his mouse-grey dressing gown and took out a deck of cards. He pulled out eight and placed them on the table between us. *Temperance, The Hermit, The Magician, Judgement, The Wheel of Fortune, The Hanged Man, The Lovers,* and *The High Priestess.* He pointed to the last.

"In most decks this card is known as The High Priestess, but it is sometimes called *La Papesse* – the female Pope, a reference to the mediaeval legend of Pope Joan, who supposedly reigned as pontiff from 855 to 857. You will recall that Mrs. Eastwick's maiden name was *Pope.*"

"Joan Pope – Pope Joan. And for that fact alone she was killed? That's insane."

"These are eight of what are known as the *Major Arcana*. In all, there are twenty-two, so if nothing is done, we may expect fourteen more killings, each of them somehow reflecting one of the cards."

And he spread them out in front of me.

The Emperor, *The Hierophant*, *The Chariot*, *Strength*, *Death*, *The Devil*, *The Tower*, *The Star*, *The Moon*, *The Sun*, *Justice*, *The World*, *The Fool*, and *The Empress*.

I confess that my imagination ran riot, wondering who our mysterious antagonist might kill for each card. Strength – a circus strongman? The Fool – a clown, or a music hall comedian? Justice – a barrister? Someone else on the Bench? The Tower – would he have someone thrown from one, or destroy one, as in the picture on the card? Perhaps even The Tower of London itself? I shuddered as I looked at the picture of The Empress. Might he even attempt the assassination of Queen Victoria, the Empress of India?

As so often, Holmes, who knew me so well, divined my thought.

"We will stop him before he has time to perpetrate any more of the horrors these crude pictures may suggest, old friend."

"I certainly hope so. What is our first move?"

"We are going to visit a member of The Order of Thoth."

The Hermetic Order of Thoth, as my companion informed me en route, was founded in 1865 by three Freemasons called William Henry Archer, Hartley Frobisher, and Michael Drax-Morton. A number of celebrated names were involved, or alleged to be involved with the organization. The rituals of The Order were influenced by a mixture of so-called magical disciplines: The Hermetic *Qabbalah*, geomancy, alchemy, astrology, and the occult interpretation of the Tarot.

"How did you come to be interested in any of this?" I asked Holmes.

"It does seem a little out of character, does it not? I came to this knowledge by a circuitous route. As you know, before we began sharing rooms in Baker Street, I lodged for some time in Montague Street, near the British Museum. Pickings were thin, and it occurred to me that if I couldn't always use my abilities in the field, I might at least make a little money by writing monographs on subjects which were germane to the profession. I have mentioned before my studies of the different types of tobacco ash and the effect of different types of labour on the contours of the human hand. Both of these were produced doing this period. There were others which I started, but, for various reasons, did not complete.

"One of these was on the subject of the different methods of cheating at cards. There would be no point in finishing it now because Maskelyne has since written the definitive text on the subject. As to the Tarot, I learned, while studying the history of cards in the Reading Room, that despite some claims that it has its origins back in the mists of antiquity, in actuality the deck can only be traced back with any certainty to mid-fifteenth century Italy. First known as '*Trionfo*', then '*Taroccho*', the cards were used to play various games. The name *Tarot* comes from the French. It wasn't until about 1780 that it began to be used as cartomancy, using the fall of the cards to predict the future."

"And this fellow that we are going to see – ?"

"Is an expert on the Tarot. In fact, he has written a book on the subject. His name is Sebastian Childe."

"You don't think he is the author of these crimes?"

"I think it extremely unlikely, but he may be able to guide us to the person who is."

After Holmes rang the bell at 23 Holland Park Grove, the door was answered by Sebastian Childe himself. He was a tall, thin man of about thirty-five with a pale face, watery blue eyes, and light blond hair. Perhaps the most notable thing about him was his air of abstraction, which evoked the feeling that he wasn't entirely engaged with mundane reality, but lived half on another more-rarified plane of existence. I could agree with Holmes that he seemed unlikely to have anything to do with anything so base as murder.

"Yes?" he inquired in a reedy voice.

"Mr. Sebastian Childe?"

"I am he, and you are – ?"

"I am Sherlock Holmes, and this is Dr. John Watson, my colleague and friend."

An expression of pure joy spread across Childe's sharp features and he seized my companion's hand and shook it.

"Mr. Holmes! Why, this is indeed an honour!"

I hadn't expected a practitioner of the occult to be so pleased to meet the foremost practical logician of his day, but Childe continued, "A positive pleasure to meet another seeker after truth, for that is what we both are, in our own ways, though we travel to it via different paths. And Dr. Watson! I have read everything you have written, and with great enjoyment. Please, please, come in, and tell me how I may assist you."

Childe ushered us into his living room. Although it was still day, the gas lamps were lit, as the tall windows were masked by thick, colourful tapestries. A piece of some lightly scented incense was burning in a metal bowl set on a tripod in the corner. The walls were covered in bookshelves which were stacked with heavy old tomes, and here and there some obviously more recent publications, all doubtless concerned with mysticism and similar topics. On almost every other flat surface – the mantelpiece, the tables, and part of the floor – there were various artifacts which reflected the occupant's interests: A foot-high Buddha which appeared to have been carved from ebony, a bronze statuette of the goddess Kali, several African idols, a nine-inch replica of the Diana of the Ephesians, and, on a small metal stand, an icon of Isis, Osiris, and Horus. Amidst all this, only one modern thing stood out: A typewriter at a small desk, which Childe, or his secretary (if he had one), doubtless used to transcribe his various writings.

At his bidding, we sat down in two capacious armchairs opposite a chaise longue.

"Would you care for some tea?" he asked, ringing the bell. "I generally take some at this time. I trust oolong is to your taste?"

A neatly dressed, petite young maid brought the tea, and Childe said, as I took my first tentative sip, "So, how may I be of assistance to the Great Detective and his associate?"

"You are an acknowledged expert on the Tarot," Holmes began.

"Thank you. I take it you have read my book, *The Tarot Explained*?"

"Yes."

"Do you have a copy? You must let me give you a signed one before you leave, if you have not."

"That is gracious of you, but let me come straight to the point. Your interpretation of the deck is that it goes back to ancient Egypt, and that it is a guide to spiritual growth."

"Yes. I spent many years researching the subject before I first put pen to paper, and I am convinced that that interpretation is the only correct one."

"That may be so, but what other interpretations are you aware of? Are there any, for example, that might countenance or encourage the use of violence?"

"A strange question. Why do you ask?"

"You are unaware of the recent rash of murders?"

"I never read newspapers, Mr. Holmes. The mundane trivialities they deal in can only distract one from contemplation of the eternal verities. But since you ask, yes, I do know of one such. Have you heard of Valentine Athlone?"

"Never."

"The better for you. It is a lamentable aspect of occult groups that they are inclined to factionalism. Individuals will disagree over the meaning of texts, the correct conduct of this or that ritual, or the necessity of keeping the workings of the group a secret from outsiders. Fortunately, The Order of Thoth was free from such divisions – or, that is, it was until the coming of Valentine Athlone. My reading of the Tarot was accepted by most of the members of The Order, except him and a few others. It became clear that he was a Satanist, that he saw the Tarot as a guide to the liberation of Lucifer and his elevation to the Lord of the Universe. He was expelled from The Order and began his own group, The Legion of Lucifer. Our Order has a distinguished membership of artists, writers, and actors. He managed to convince a few of us, the weaker ones, the ones less sure in our truth, to join him, but for the most part his Legion is a cesspool of drug addicts and criminals. Let me show you a copy of his book, in which I believe he advocates human sacrifice."

He stood, went over to one of the crowded bookshelves, and took out a slim volume which bore the title *The Book of Lucifer*.

"It is an almost unreadable mixture of bad poetry, prose poems, and tortuous Satanic utterances, but look at this page."

He opened the book and handed it to Holmes. I leaned over to look. It read:

The Coming Age is The Age of Lucifer!
Tremble, O ye Christians, mired in repression and fear!
Tremble, O ye Muslims, in your base servitude!
Tremble, O ye Jews, in your temples of greed!
Tremble, O ye Hindus, in your dark and childish ways!
Tremble, O ye Atheists, deniers of His light!
For the Coming Age is The Age of Lucifer!
He rises once more from the ancient prison!
All earth shall bow to His thought!
Intellect shall rule over base emotion!
For His way is the way of the mind!
What must be done shall be done!
O, the Coming Age is The Age of Lucifer! "

On the Tarot
The ancient Tarot, first formed by the sages of Egypt and passed down the centuries to us, is more, has more power, than any other single talisman on earth. Some have called it a mere game, others a guidebook for the progress of the soul. I alone have uncovered its true secret. When the Catholic Church dubbed it the Devil's Picture Book, they were more correct than they knew. By the correct use of the Tarot, we can expedite the ascension of Lucifer to His rightful place on the glorious throne.

The way will be hard and bloody, and beset by the dull morality of the unbelievers. It will mean sacrifice for each of the twenty-two cards of the Major Arcana, *but when it is done and we are steeped in blood, then shall Lucifer return, for the Coming Age is The Age of Lucifer!*

The superior man shall rise, and the inferior man shall fall, for the Coming Age is The Age of Lucifer!

"These are the ravings of a madman!" I cried.

"Perhaps," said Holmes, "but there is nothing more dangerous than a madman who believes himself to be sane – saner, indeed, than all others. Mr. Childe, do you have Athlone's address?"

"You will find it in the book."

"May we take it?"

"Certainly, but – "

"I rather fear that Athlone has already begun his campaign of death. Come, Watson, there's no time to lose!"

"Your signed copy of my book – " Childe began.

"Send it to me. I think you know the address."

We rushed out into the street and hailed the first passing hansom.

"Scotland Yard!" cried Holmes as we clambered inside.

As may be imagined, the prosaic, stolid Scotland Yarders at first found it difficult to believe that the unprepossessing, badly printed little volume that Holmes presented to them could possibly contain the key to a series of unsolved murders. But during his long absence, it had become clear how valuable his methods were, and how keenly he was missed. His stock among the Force was high, and it wasn't long before a detective and two constables were dispatched to bring Valentine Athlone in for questioning. He proved to be a tall, dark-haired young man whose characteristic expression was a sneer of aristocratic disdain.

While he was being held at Bow Street Police Station, Inspectors Gregson and Lestrade acquired a warrant to search Athlone's house in Highgate. Holmes and I were permitted to accompany them, and there the four of us found ample evidence of Athlone's guilt.

The house, as well as having rooms adapted for various Satanic rituals, also contained information gathered by Athlone's Legion regarding the victims – newspaper clippings, transcriptions of gossip, names copied from electoral registers, dates and times, theatrical programmes, legal reports, and more. All evidence that the victims had been meticulously researched and chosen.

It was then that the diligence of the professionals came into play. By unstinting hard work, they eventually had the names and addresses of all the members of The Legion of Lucifer and a good grasp of the extent to which each one was involved in The Legion's terrible crimes. So the praise they received from the judge was well deserved, but as so often, without the help of Mr. Sherlock Holmes, they would have remained forever in the dark.

The Conk-Singleton Forgery

In her youth, Lady Lydia Conk-Singleton had been a noted beauty, and even now, well into her sixth decade, she was still an exceptionally handsome woman. Indeed, part of her attraction was that she had allowed herself to age naturally, without recourse to the dyes and heavy make-up so often resorted to by ladies of a certain age. Her hair was a little touched with grey, and her delicately featured face was pale. Nature had provided her with an erect carriage and a slim form, which she retained, despite having given birth to two children. Her husband, Lord Alfred Conk-Singleton, was some twenty years her senior. There were those who had expressed disbelief that he was finally giving up his bachelorhood, and presumed that he had married her because the necessity for an heir was pressing. Others found the match questionable, not only because of the difference in their ages, but also because Lydia Lilburn was the daughter of a northern industrialist rather than a product of the nobility.

But it wasn't long before all such doubts and reservations were summarily dispelled by the obvious and absolute devotion which existed between the couple. As well as serving as a shining example of marital harmony, their administration of the extensive Conk-Singleton estates was a model of aristocratic responsibility. They maintained the rents at a reasonable and affordable level and cared for their tenants, who knew that if they were in financial difficulties, or had other troubles, they could always look to the big house for help. In addition, the Conk-Singletons kept the parish church and the local school in good repair, despite the fact that there was no onus upon them to do so.

It was somewhat of a surprise, then, for both Sherlock Holmes and myself, when we received a telegram from the lady in question, informing us that she would call on us at eleven o'clock that morning on a matter of extreme delicacy and importance. What might have happened, we both wondered, to disturb the even tenor of their lives?

Lady Lydia entered our sitting room at exactly the stated time, clad in an elegant dove-grey ensemble. She took a seat opposite us and removed her kid gloves.

"Good morning, Lady Lydia," said Holmes. "You are most prompt. Would you care for some tea?"

"No, thank you, Mr. Holmes."

"You may go, Mrs. Hudson."

Having ushered the lady in, our housekeeper had hovered by the door in anticipation of Holmes's offer of refreshment.

"Now," said the detective as Mrs. Hudson's footsteps padded down the stairs, "how may Dr. Watson and I be of assistance to you?"

"Have you heard of Lord John Fleming?"

Holmes's thin lips pursed in distaste, and I fancy that my own expression must have displayed the extreme loathing that any decent person felt at the very mention of the fellow's name. An inveterate gambler and undoubtedly a cheat, married but an unscrupulous womanizer, he was one of the very worst men in London. He had investments in the Congo Free State and supported Leopold II's tyrannical regime in that unfortunate colony. There were even rumours, largely unsubstantiated, that he was a practising Satanist who carried out unspeakable rites of black magic at his crumbling ancestral manor in Cornwall.

"Oh, I have heard of him," said Holmes, "and considered it only a matter of time before our paths must cross. But what have you to do with such an arrant scoundrel?"

"In order to answer that question, I must go back some way into my husband's family history."

"Please proceed. I take it you will not object if Dr. Watson takes notes?"

"Not at all. It is common knowledge that the first Lord Singleton was given Hemsworth Hall, and all the lands that go with it, by Henry VII, as a reward for supporting the king at the Battle of Bosworth Field in 1485. The house was renamed Conk-Singleton Hall when the third Lord married the Duchess of Conques from southern France and combined their titles.

"In 1720, as a result of investing in the South Sea Company – which, as you may know, had a disastrous collapse – the tenth Lord Conk-Singleton's wealth was drastically reduced. In 1750, his grandson attempted to restore the family fortunes by sinking their remaining money into tea. By this time it had become the national drink, and clipper ships were making regular journeys between England and India and China. The twelfth Lord had purchased three such ships and, unfortunately they were several weeks overdue. They and their cargo were insured, but there must be definite report of their loss before the insurance company would pay up, and his creditors were becoming insistent.

"Alfred's ancestor borrowed a considerable amount to pay them off. But the man who supplied the money was one Lord Augustus Fleming, who up to that point Lord Conk-Singleton had considered a friend. Fleming took advantage of the twelfth Lord's fear of ruin and dishonour. He demanded the house and estates, which were worth at least ten times what was owed, as collateral against the debt. Should the clippers not return before a certain date, and bearing a cargo of sufficient value to cover the debt, Conk-Singleton Hall, and, as they say, 'all the lands appertaining thereto' would become the property of Lord Augustus Fleming."

"But clearly," I said, "that didn't happen."

"No. Lord Fleming disappeared shortly before the due date. Inevitably, some people claimed that Lord Conk-Singleton had murdered him, or had had him murdered. Fleming was addicted to gambling and brothels, so others thought he'd been killed in some vile den and his body tossed in the Thames."

"I have two questions," said Holmes. "First, was there any documentation, and does it survive? And second, Fleming must have had an heir – presumably Lord John's ancestor."

"I know of no surviving documentation, but Fleming claims to have a deed signed by the twelfth Lord acknowledging that he has failed to meet the conditions of the bond, and transferring ownership of the house and estate to Lord Augustus Fleming and his heirs in perpetuity. Signed by both parties. Alfred consulted his solicitor, and if genuine, it still has the force of law."

"There would have been a record at the Port Authority stating when the ships came in."

"Gone, though it isn't clear when. It doesn't seem to have occurred to Fleming's heir to try and track it down. He was Augustus Fleming's nephew, about seven years old when his uncle died, and living with his widowed mother, Fleming's sister-in-law, on a remote Scottish island. He was in his mid-twenties before he heard about any of this."

"There will still have to be civil proceedings before anything can be settled."

"I don't want that to happen, Mr. Holmes. I am here by myself because my husband is now seventy years old and in poor health. I'm not sure that his constitution could stand the strain of a public exposure of a stain on his ancestor's character. I dare not think what would follow if this document is upheld. We have said nothing to our children. How are we to tell them that they might lose their inheritance? And then there are our tenants. What will happen to them if the estate falls into Fleming's hands? I have no doubt that he will bleed them dry, raise the rents, and refuse to give them any assistance of any kind, whatever trouble they are in. The parish church is older than the Hall itself. Will a man like that do anything for its upkeep? You must help us, Mr. Holmes, Dr. Watson! You must! You must!"

Lady Lydia's aristocratic demeanour broke down in that instant, and tears welled in her eyes. I was about to go for my medical bag and obtain a sedative, but Holmes reached across to her, and she didn't demur as he took her hand in both of his and spoke in a soothing tone.

"Lady Conk-Singleton, you may rest assured that both my friend and I will do all we can to thwart this villain's plans. But what is there for us to do?"

The lady gently withdrew her hand and, after dabbing briefly at her eyes with a monogrammed white handkerchief, regained her composure.

"I apologise, gentlemen. There is one hope: We have the legal right to have the document examined by an independent agent, and as I have been informed that you have an expertise in these matters, I should like you, Mr. Holmes, to be that agent. Surely you can determine whether it is genuine or a forgery."

"I shall certainly do my utmost."

"We shall reward you handsomely, come what may."

"For the moment, I would merely ask you to defray any trifling expenses we may incur in the course of the investigation. Any additional payment you may care to make if the case is successfully concluded will be at your discretion. Now, I assume that this document is in the hands of Lord Fleming's solicitors. Their name and address?"

"Melmoth and Poole, 14 Old Fish Street, E.C. I shall arrange an appointment for you via my solicitors, Pettifer and Treadgold."

"We shall await your notification."

Lady Conk-Singleton rose.

"Thank you, gentlemen. I feel much better, knowing the matter is in your hands."

The head partner of Melmoth and Poole, Solicitors, of 14, Old Fish St, London E.C., was Sir Cecil Melmoth, a dry, cadaverous individual whose prevailing vice seemed to be the use of snuff. He sniffed a pinch of the powder into each flaring nostril of his hawk's bill of a nose and looked somewhat disdainfully across his desk at the three visitors whose arrival had upset the placid order of his morning. One of them he doubtless recognised as Donald Sedge, a junior partner in the firm of Pettifer and Treadgold.

"Sir Cecil," said Sedge, "allow me to introduce Mr. Sherlock Holmes and Dr. John H. Watson."

"Pleased to make your acquaintance, I'm sure."

"We understand that as you are Lord John Fleming's solicitors, he has left the document attesting to his ownership of Conk-Singleton Hall and its lands in your keeping."

"That is correct, Mr. Sedge."

"Mr. Holmes and Dr. Watson are here on behalf of Lord and Lady Conk-Singleton. You may have heard of them. They have assisted Scotland Yard in the solution of crimes, and the apprehension of criminals."

"I'm sorry, the names mean nothing to me. Nor do I see how any assistance they may have given to the police has any bearing on a civil case."

"Sir Cecil," said Holmes, "I'm sure you would concede that in a case of this kind, the provenance of such a document is of the highest importance, especially when so much property is in question, and after such a long time. Where was the document found?"

"At Fleming House, in an old box in a drawer containing several other papers from the same period. The box was locked and had clearly lain unopened for many years."

"Were there any others present when the box was found?"

"Lord John's wife and brother. They were also present when it was opened."

"I see."

"I thought you had a request, rather than questions. What is it?"

"We wish, as legal agents for Lord and Lady Conk-Singleton, to examine the document to ascertain whether or not it is a forgery."

"Ah," said Sir Cecil, "Lord John suspected that someone acting on behalf of the Conk-Singletons would make such a request, and, under my advisement, he is prepared to allow it – provided some conditions are met."

"Which are?"

"Firstly, that the person making such examination must do so here in these offices, in the presence of two or more witnesses appointed by his legal representatives. In other words, by us."

"I acknowledge your right to make that condition," said Holmes.

"At no point is the document to leave the sight of said witnesses."

"Agreed."

"Only one agent of the Conk-Singletons is allowed to be here in our premises to examine said document. Given that this chap here seems incapable of speech – " He looked over at me contemptuously. " – I'm assuming that will be you – What was your name again?"

"Sherlock Holmes."

Donald Sedge departed to walk the short distance back to the offices of Pettifer and Treadgold and Holmes and I hailed a cab to Baker Street

"I am afraid that Sir Cecil Melmoth is well within the law in insisting on such conditions," said Holmes as our vehicle rattled through the cobbled streets of the City, "but you may rest assured that I shall give you a full report when I return from their offices tomorrow afternoon. Now, I don't know about you, but I suddenly feel a distinct need to drive the atmosphere of Number 14, Old Fish Street from my system. The Reichmann Quartet are playing in – " He consulted his pocket watch. " – twenty minutes, and I find that there is nothing like the sound of stringed instruments in harmony to sooth and invigorate the mind."

He raised his stick and thumped the roof of the vehicle.

"Cabby!"

"Yes, sir?"

"A change of destination. Wigmore Hall, and an extra five shillings for you if you can get us there before three o'clock."

Hans Reichmann and his three associates were indeed in fine form on that spring afternoon, and, as they embarked on the opening movement of Cherubini's *Second Quartet in C Major*, I turned to look at my friend as he sat, eyes closed and chin slightly lifted, totally absorbed in the performance. I marvelled, for perhaps the hundredth time, at the strange multiplicity of his nature. How, for example, the man who relentlessly pursued the criminal as the hunter pursued the beasts of the jungle might transform thence into the thinking machine whose keen logic saw through the machinations of lesser men, or into the being beside me, who could be transported to some other realm by the sublimity of music, and how, in some unfathomable fashion, each of these personae supported and strengthened the others.

The day continued in pleasant manner. We returned to our lodgings and had a splendid dinner, after which we sat and chatted in an aimless and desultory manner on various subjects – possible treatments for colour blindness, the early history of the papacy, the work of Joseph Bazalgette, and the poetry of Francois Villon – until, at about ten in the evening, Holmes stood up and glanced at the clock.

"I must bid you goodnight, Watson, for I suspect that tomorrow will tax my patience as well as my intellect, and I would be well rested."

As may be imagined, when Holmes returned late in the following afternoon, I was eager to learn what flaws he had found in the old document, and how the odious Fleming would be prevented from seizing the Conk-Singleton house and estates. But as he entered our living-room, it was immediately obvious that his examination hadn't been a successful one. I said nothing as he threw himself down into his customary armchair with a sigh and pulled his pipe from his pocket. I silently handed him his Persian slipper and waited as he filled the bowl and applied a match to it. The first few inhalations of smoke seemed to lighten his mood a little.

"Watson", he said, "what do you know about the falsification of documents?"

"Nothing at all," I replied. "You have yet to write a monograph on the subject."

"Don't pretend that you spend any time reading my little efforts. Do you remember what you said about *The Book of Life*, the first one you ever saw?"

"As I recall, I called it the product of an armchair lounger whose theories wouldn't stand up if he attempted to put them to practical use, or words to that effect. But we have both come a long way since then."

"Then you have read them?"

"Well, I've glanced at one or two."

I was pleased to hear Holmes give a short barking laugh.

"Ha! I've had a frustrating day, and part of my irritation was that my old friend wasn't there to provide me with a sounding-board."

"I'm here now, Holmes, and you were about to enlighten me regarding the forgery of documents."

"So I was. Firstly, there is the material upon which the document is written or printed. Old vellum which hasn't been written on isn't so easy to come by these days, and it is relatively simple to discern if something is a palimpsest – that is to say, a piece from which the top layer, and the writing on it, have been scraped away and replaced by a different text. Fresh vellum is too obviously new to serve the forger's turn. In any case, the document was written on paper. I should have liked to take a flake of the page and examine it under the microscope, but I wouldn't have been allowed to do so. The paper had no watermark by which it could be dated, but it appeared to be of genuine eighteenth-century manufacture.

"Then there is the writing itself. Everyone's handwriting is ultimately based on the way they were taught at school, and the script children were taught a century or two ago is different from that which you and I use. However, my examination revealed no significant variations from the standard style of the eighteenth century. Next comes the ink. The ink of the period was made of a few very simple ingredients. In fact, many people made their own. Again, if I could have examined it under a microscope, I would have seen whether or not it contained any modern elements.

"Staying with the writing, we must consider the spelling and the style. Once more, I found nothing to arouse my suspicions. Last of all, there are the signatures, purporting to be those of the twelfth Lord Conk-Singleton and Lord Augustus Fleming. If either one of those could be proved false, it would invalidate the entire document. But with only one example of each signature, how was I to prove either false?

"I received permission to make a copy of the document, which I have here."

He produced a folded sheet of paper from the inside pocket of his jacket.

"I made a particular effort to reproduce the signatures as accurately as possible, and I flatter myself I did a fine job of it. Do you know where I took it to find signatures with which to compare my copies?"

"Somerset House?"

"Not a bad guess, but no. Fleming and Conk-Singleton were both aristocrats, members of the House of Lords, and I felt there were bound to be examples of their signatures in the archives of the Houses of Parliament. Normally one would need an appointment, but fortunately Cavendish, the archivist, was indebted to me because I had once disproved an allegation of theft which was made against him."

"Cavendish? I don't recall the name."

"It was before your time. I was still in Montague Street. My surmise was correct. Lord Conk-Singleton's signature on the document didn't seem to be exactly the same as that on a memorandum in the archive. Cavendish politely explained, however, that one's handwriting might change, temporarily or permanently, due to illness or old age. Were it not for the fact that he has been in Pentonville Prison for the last eight years, I might have thought it the work of our old friend Victor Lynch, had he decided to move from currency to documents. I am still convinced that it is a forgery. It would need an expert, or a team of experts, to carry it off, but it is far from impossible."

"How would it be done?"

"First you get an old, blank sheet of paper from the eighteenth century. There are plenty of them in existence. A page from the back of an old book, for example, where the text didn't run to the end of the section. Mix up a batch of ink using simple ingredients. Copy the script style and the writing style from books or magazines of the period – there are enough of those around, too. As to the difference between the two Conk-Singleton signatures, I can even explain that in another way to Cavendish. The signature on the document was shakier than the one in the archive. The document was written in 1752. Conk-Singleton was thirty-seven then, but his signature in the archive came from 1779, when he was sixty-four, and it was firm and clear. He died in 1792 at the age of seventy-seven. Yes, it's possible that he was ill when he signed the document, but supposing he wasn't?

"The main problem with forging signatures, or handwriting, is hesitation. It is difficult to produce something that flows in the way that the genuine article does. But this can be overcome, though the process is long and tedious. If you practice over and over again, eventually you will reach a point where you can produce a reasonable copy spontaneously. What's happened here, I think, is that the forger has done his practice, but the example he had to copy was from very late in Conk-Singleton's life, when his signature had become shaky."

"But we cannot prove any of this."

"No. But there must be something. I will re-examine this copy, and if I find nothing there, I will look at the original again tomorrow."

"Will Sir Cecil Melmoth let you?"

"Oh, I don't doubt he will puff and bluster, but the law is on my side. Remember, I am the Conk-Singletons' designated agent. I must have access to it until the civil case comes to court."

"Watson! Watson! Wake up, old chap!"

"What? What is it?"

Mrs. Hudson had cooked us a particularly fine dinner, accompanied by an excellent Chablis, and shortly after we had finished, I seem to have drifted into a light sleep.

I rubbed my eyes and saw Holmes standing before me, his face wreathed in a smile of triumph.

"Watson, luck has been on our side!"

"Luck? You have always said that a detective should never rely on luck."

"Nor should he, but when luck goes his way, he would be foolish not to take advantage of the fact."

"You've solved the secret of the forgery."

"I have indeed. I should have seen it from the very first."

"Are you going to tell me?"

Holmes's grin become positively impish.

"I think I shall take a hint from your fantastic little tales and leave the revelation until the *denouement.* In the meantime, here is my copy of the document. See what you can make of it."

"I don't need to look at the original?"

"No, no, the answer is there in front of you."

I looked at the sheet again and again but was unable to see what Holmes was driving at. After an hour, I gave up the attempt and took myself to bed.

The following afternoon found us once more at the offices of Messrs. Melmoth and Poole, nestled in one of the more archaic back streets of the City, where fish had once been on sale. Also present were Lady Conk-Singleton, Sir Cecil Melmoth, Donald Sedge, Lord John Fleming, his brother George, and his wife Lucy.

"I have complied with your wishes, Mr. Holmes, and with those of Lady Conk-Singleton," said Sir Cecil, "but this is very irregular."

"Irregular, but necessary," said Holmes. "I have irrefutable proof that the document Lord Fleming claims entitles him to the Conk-Singleton manor house and estates is nothing but a forgery."

"Impossible!" bellowed Fleming. He was a giant of a man with a heavy black beard and a red, choleric face. "The drawer containing that box with the document was opened for the first time in centuries, in front of witnesses."

"Witnesses? Your brother and your wife? Hardly impartial, or unimpeachable."

"You can't prove it's a fake, damn you!"

"Meaning it is one?"

Sir Cecil Melmoth paused in the middle of taking a pinch of snuff.

"Lord John," he said wearily, "you are doing your case no good with these outbursts. And you, sir – Mr. Holmes – please come to the point."

"I shall very shortly, Sir Cecil, but first, I must ask your indulgence while I deliver a short history lecture. In October 1582, Pope Gregory XIII introduced the Gregorian calendar to replace the Julian calendar, which had miscalculated the length of the year by eleven minutes. Over the course of the centuries this had resulted in the date of the vernal equinox, which marked – "

"What the d----d Hell is this?" blustered Fleming. "The date of the document is *1752*, not *1582*!"

"As I said before, if you will please indulge me, the relevance will soon become clear."

Fleming's face flushed a brighter red and he sat back with a sour expression, but remained silent.

"Thank you, Lord John. Now, this error meant that the vernal equinox, which marked the first day of spring, was far too close to the traditional dates calculated for Easter. To correct this situation, Gregory excised eleven days from the month of October 1582. While this reform was accepted throughout the Catholic countries, the Protestant states rejected it, partly because it was a considered a Papist heresy and partly because it would create confusion over the correct time for the celebration of Christmas. But eventually, over one-hundred-fifty years later, Protestant countries began to accept it.

"Britain was almost the last to adopt the Gregorian system, and it is said that when the days were excised from the year, uneducated folk rioted, demanding, 'Give us back our eleven days!' This story is often told by those who love to depict the common man as irredeemably stupid, but if these riots did take place, it was probably because people were justifiably afraid that they would have to pay a full month's rent while only being paid for the smaller number of days they had worked that month. Now, Sir Cecil, I understand that the document has been placed once more in your safe. Would you do me the courtesy of removing it?"

The aged solicitor stood and went to the steel safe standing at the back of the room and opened it, carefully shielding the combination from everyone else.

He took out a manila folder and handed it to Holmes, who rose, turned back the flap, and passed it to Fleming.

"This is your document, sir?"

"You know damn well it is!"

"In that case, would you read out the date at the top, please."

"The eighth of September, 1752. What of it?"

"It may interest you to know that the year in which eleven days were finally excised from the British calendar was 1752. The month was September, the days in question being the 3rd to the 13th of that month. Could you explain to us all how this document came to be written and signed on a day that didn't exist?"

Fleming flung the paper to the floor with a snarl and rose from his chair, his face scarlet with anger, his powerful bulky body towering over Holmes.

"Well?" said the detective. "Can you?"

There was a firm knock at the door. I stood and opened it to reveal the familiar face of Inspector Lestrade, who was accompanied by two burly uniformed constables.

"Ah, good afternoon, Inspector. I trust you haven't been waiting long."

"Good to see you, Mr. Holmes. And you too, of course, Doctor. I got your note and came at once. Now, Lord John Fleming, I must ask you and your wife and brother to accompany myself and Constables Barnaby and Callaghan to Scotland Yard to be questioned on the matters of fraud and attempted extortion."

For a moment it seemed that Fleming was sizing up Barnaby and Callaghan to see if there was any chance that he could take them down and make his escape.

"Don't try it, Lord John," Lestrade said gently. "You wouldn't last two minutes. Come quietly. Cuff them, Barnaby."

Holmes bent down, picked up the document, and handed it to the Scotland Yarder.

"Evidence?" asked the inspector.

"Yes. It was evidence that Fleming thought would secure him a fortune, but now it's evidence that will send him to prison. His accomplices too, if you can find them."

Fleming lunged towards Holmes, but Callaghan and Barnaby seized an arm each and held him back.

"I'll break you, Holmes!" he screamed. "I'll snap you like a rotten twig!"

"So many have said so, but here I am, still unbroken."

"There's a Black Maria outside for you three," said Lestrade. "Let's not keep her waiting any longer."

Sir Cecil Melmoth reached into his waistcoat pocket and once more took out his little tin of snuff.

"Thank you for arranging this meeting at such short notice," said Holmes.

"You're welcome," said Sir Cecil, and sniffed up two pinches of the brown powder. "I underestimated you, Mr. Holmes, and for that I must apologise. There were a few other papers in that box of Sir John's. Might I ask you to take a look at them to check their authenticity? For your standard fee, of course."

"I would be happy to."

"Good. I shall send them 'round to you by courier tomorrow afternoon. Your address?"

"221b Baker Street."

It was pleasant to be outside once more in the spring sunshine.

Lady Lydia Conk-Singleton took the detective by the hand and said, "Thank you, thank you, Mr. Holmes! You have given our children back their future, saved our tenants, and lifted the clouds that loured upon our house. My husband can live out his remaining years in peace. All this is due to you, and here is a small token of my gratitude."

She reached inside her reticule and withdrew a folded cheque. Holmes opened it and said, "My Lady, this is most generous."

"'*The labourer is more than worthy of his hire.*' Now, here is my carriage. May I take you gentlemen back to Baker Street?"

The following day, Holmes was deeply involved in some abstruse chemical experiment when a thought struck me.

"Holmes?"

"What?"

"Something disturbing has occurred to me."

He swung round in his chair, a foaming beaker in his right hand.

"And what might that be?"

"There is no proof that the twelfth Lord Conk-Singleton's clippers actually *did* return to England in time for him to repay his debt."

"True enough."

"And for all we know, Conk-Singleton's ancestor may have actually had Lord Augustus Fleming killed."

"Again, that is undeniably possible, but what of it?"

"Lord John Fleming's claim to the manor and estates may have been justified."

"Possibly, but would you have preferred that he had won the case?"

"Well, no, of course not."

"Then I suggest that you do not let it trouble your conscience, as I certainly don't intend to let it trouble mine. Do you know the philosophical conundrum of the drunkard with a hundred gold pieces?"

"I don't believe so."

"A drunkard has a hundred gold pieces, which he plans to spend on drink. Another man comes and steals his money, and distributes it to the poor. Who has the right of it?"

"Very well. I take your point."

The Adventure of the Elfrincham Maze

The events surrounding the death of Edward Crawley in the hedge maze at Elfrincham, West Sussex, are no longer fresh in the public mind, and may therefore serve as the basis for the following narrative, which reveals, for the first time, the part played in the case by my friend, Mr. Sherlock Holmes, and, to a somewhat lesser degree, by myself.

It was a beautiful, sunny morning in late June. From the window of our sitting room in Baker Street, I looked down to see young couples stopping before the shop windows, the men dapper in their summer suits, the young women bright as new blooms in their gaily coloured dresses. No one abroad in the thoroughfare that day seemed to be in a hurry. The traffic was full but not heavy, and even the tradesmen in their carts seemed content to amble on at little more than a snail's pace. The sun beamed down on rich and poor alike, and while there was undoubtedly work to be done, its warm rays imparted a holiday atmosphere to the day's proceedings. In all, it seemed an improbable venue for the consideration of such things as murder, but having lodged with the world's first consulting detective for some years, I had become accustomed to the fact that violence and crime could rear their heads in the unlikeliest of circumstances.

The morning's glad sunshine was certainly no guarantee that all was right in the world.

Holmes was in the midst of composing a short, bright piece for violin. The mid-morning had been punctuated by little bursts of music, between which he wrote or crossed out notation on the sheet before him on his desk. I sat in my usual armchair and picked up one of H. Rider Haggard's fine adventure stories set in the African veldt.

Mrs. Hudson entered with a telegram for Holmes, who seized it eagerly and, after running his eyes over it, gave a bark of satisfaction.

"Ha! Thank you, Mrs. Hudson."

As our landlady turned to go, Holmes smiled at me and said, "Well, Watson, it is as I expected," and passed me the message. I put my book down. The telegram read:

> *Elfrincham Maze case proving a puzzle. Would be grateful if you could come down to assist. Have booked rooms for you and Dr. Watson at Crown Hotel in High Street.*
>
> *Inspector Walcott*
> *West Sussex Constabulary*

"Walcott is a sound fellow, if a little slow," said Holmes. "You may recall, he brought us in over that business in Arundel Castle."

"The theft of the Gainsborough?"

"Exactly. Now, my friend, what do you know of this Elfrincham affair?"

"Only that Edward Crawley was found dead at the centre of the maze."

Holmes took a slim volume from his desk.

"I picked this up in Paternoster Row yesterday afternoon," he said, handing it to me. "It will provide you with all the information you need to understand the background to the case."

I looked at the spine. It read: *The Hedge Mazes of England* by H.R. Kitson.

"A train leaves from Victoria Station in – " He glanced over at the clock on the mantelpiece. " – forty minutes. I'm sure ten minutes will suffice for you to gather all the necessaries for our little trip, so I shall meet you downstairs at a quarter-past-eleven."

Soon we were ensconced in a comfortable smoking carriage on the 11:45 to West Worthing. Holmes was immersed in the last two days' newspapers, so I opened the little book by H.R. Kitson to the chapter on the Elfrincham Maze and read:

> *The hedge maze in the grounds of Elfrincham Manor in West Sussex has not achieved the same measure of fame as, for example, the celebrated maze at Hampton Court, despite its being the largest and most complex such maze in England. There are two probable reasons for this: Firstly, it was originally*

planted in 1594 but has not been in continuous existence since then, having been destroyed by fire in mysterious circumstances in 1726. It was replanted in 1797 in accordance with the original ground plan. Secondly, it has never been open to the general public.

A tradition was established in 1810 whereby, on the weekend of or before each Midsummer's Day, exactly forty guests are invited to stay at the manor, and from those forty, four men and four women are chosen by lot to enter the maze at sunset. The lots are kept in two large leather bags, one for the men and one for the women, which have been replaced a few times over the years, but the majority of the wooden lots date back at least as far as the replanting. They are simple wooden discs, and four in each bag have a star painted on them. First a man picks from their bag, and then one of the women from the other, until all eight starred discs have been taken out, and then they are paired off according to the order in which the discs were picked.

The maze has five entrances. One man and one woman go in at each of four of the entrances, and the first couple to emerge from the fifth, which faces the doors of the manor house, are proclaimed King and Queen of the Maze for that year. Famous past winners include Lord Byron in 1813 (accompanied by Lady Anthea Brigstock), and Lord Balmoral and the

Duchess of Abergavenny in 1865. The tradition has continued to this day, despite the purchase of Elfrincham Manor by Lord and Lady Caerphilly from its original owners, the FitzAlwyn family, in 1881.

The rest of the chapter went on at some length about the exact species of hedge used in the planting and replanting of the maze, and the similarities and differences between the Elfrincham Maze and others in England and on the Continent, in terms of the difficulty of their solutions and the nature of the patterns they formed. Before I had reached the end of this discussion I closed the book, as I deemed that such facts were unlikely to have any bearing on the solution of the case. It was enough that I had learned that since it had been Midsummer's Day the previous weekend, Edward Crawley must have been participating in the contest of the maze when he was killed.

Holmes had dispatched a telegram to Inspector Walcott just before we had left, so when we arrived at West Worthing he was waiting for us with a dogcart. Walcott was a tall, beefy man, slow of speech, with an amiable, open expression on his broad, rubicund face. He shook us both warmly by the hand and thanked us for coming. He was, as Holmes had said, a sound fellow, but while I had no doubt that his solid physique was an asset when it came to dealing with the type of criminal he was most likely to encounter, I recalled from the Arundel Castle case that he was a little lacking in that faculty of imagination that Holmes considered an essential factor in the art of detection.

"Elfrincham isn't too far from here," Walcott said as we climbed into the cart. "About fifteen minutes, and then only about another five to the manor."

"I should like to examine the scene as soon as possible," said Holmes.

"Begging your pardon, Mr. Holmes, but the young woman who found the body is also staying at The Crown. She has to leave later today, as she's taking ship to America tomorrow. I was sure you'd want to speak to her."

"I would. Is she leaving for good?"

"No, she's visiting relatives in New York. She's given me a signed affidavit. And don't worry, I've made sure the scene remains undisturbed."

Holmes looked in my direction with a rueful little smile. I knew he had little faith in the ability of the police to leave the location of a crime untouched, but at the same time he didn't wish to malign the well-meaning Walcott.

A few minutes later we arrived at The Crown, a rather more impressive establishment than one would expect, considering the size of the village and, after depositing our luggage in our respective rooms, we were taken by Walcott to see Victoria Pryce-Jones.

She was a slim, pretty young woman with an abundance of thick, wavy brown hair braided into a long plait which hung over her left shoulder. I sensed that she possessed a natural vivacity which was still somewhat suppressed by the shock she had sustained a couple of days before. It is no small thing to be in the presence of a dead body, especially when one is aware that a life has left its mortal shell as a result of violence.

"Mr. Holmes! Dr. Watson!" she exclaimed. "I am so glad that you have come! Inspector Walcott told me you would be here. If anyone can solve this terrible crime, it is surely you. I am ready to answer any and all of your questions."

Holmes nodded. "My first question must be: Why are you staying at this hotel? Surely, as a participant in the maze game, you could be at the manor house. It has fifty guest rooms, or so I read, and the players traditionally stay for a few days after the King and Queen of the Maze have been honoured."

"That is so, but I could stay there no longer, Mr. Holmes. To awake every morning and see the maze – to be reminded of the horror I found there – was more than I could bear."

"I see. Now, Miss Pryce-Jones, I have some of the facts, but I would be obliged if you could take us through the events of that evening. Pray give us as many of the details as you can, then we'll trouble you no longer and you can prepare for your journey."

We sat on the four chairs in Miss Pryce-Jones' hotel room, and the mid-afternoon sun illumined her face as she began.

"As you may know, the game begins when the sun goes down. Eight people are chosen by lot, and I was one of them. The other seven were Johnny Faulconbridge – that is, Lord Faulconbridge – Lady Vanessa Hart, Sir Michael Rutledge, Katie, the Duchess of Belminster, Max Chesterfield, Helena Broughton, and, of course, poor Edward. That's how we were paired: Johnny and myself, Vanessa and Michael, Katie and Max, and Edward and Helena. At the centre of the maze there is a circular space about fifteen feet in diameter, and of course, as soon as you reach it, *if* you reach it, you know that you're about halfway through, which gives you some idea of how long it should take you to finish. Of course, there's no guarantee that you're the first couple to reach it, or that you'll be King and Queen."

"What happens if you meet another couple at the centre?" I asked.

"Well then, there are two other openings on the other side of the centre, and each pair goes into one. I suppose it's possible that three or even all of the couples could get to the centre at the same time, but as far as I know it's never happened. Johnny and I reached the centre pretty quickly, and we were about to congratulate ourselves on how well we were doing, when I heard a sort of low moan. Johnny had heard it too. We moved further into the center and found Edward and Helena. The maze is well lit. We saw Edward lying on his back, his shirtfront was covered in blood, and – and – " She wiped away a sudden tear with the back of her hand. "His eyes were staring upward and he had a ghastly look on his face."

Her voice became quieter. "I don't think I'll ever, ever forget that look."

"Are you all right, Miss Pryce-Jones?" I asked. "We could ring for someone to bring you a coffee, or something stronger, if you'd prefer."

"No, I – Yes, please, I'd like some water. There's a glass and a carafe by the bedside."

Walcott went over and poured her a glass. She accepted it gratefully and drank half of the contents before continuing.

"Helena was lying beside him, and there was blood on the front of her dress. She was face down, and on the back of her head you could see through her hair that there was a huge, discoloured swelling. The low moan had come from her, so we knew that she at least was alive. Johnny and I discussed what we should do and decided that since I was younger and fitter than him, I should run through the other half of the maze as quickly as I could and alert everyone waiting at the entrance. Johnny would stay in the centre to look after Helena if she woke up and tell the others what had happened when they reached the centre.

"The next twenty minutes were a nightmare. I made two or three wrong turns. and my heart was pounding so hard that I thought every minute it would burst, but eventually I made my way out. Between the entrance to the maze and the doors of the manor house, a marquee had been set up. The other thirty-two guests were sitting, drinking at little tables. As I emerged, a band struck up and, at a signal from Lord Caerphilly, the night sky was suddenly full of exploding fireworks. Even the servants were all there to see the display. I had to walk the twenty yards to where Lord and Lady Caerphilly sat, but by the time I was ten yards away he saw the expression on my face, and realizing something must be wrong, sent one of his men to tell the orchestra to stop, and that there must be no more fireworks. After I gave him the terrible news, he sent another servant to Elfrincham Village for the local doctor. All the guests and the staff went back inside the house."

"How many people know the layout of the maze?" asked Holmes.

"I imagine Lord Caerphilly must have a plan of it, but I doubt he knows it without that. Of course, the maze has to be maintained, and the gardeners who do that must know the simplest way to get through it. In fact, when the doctor arrived, Lord Caerphilly sent one of them with him, to take him through – and help the other six players out."

"Have these gardeners been questioned?" asked Holmes.

"No," said Walcott.

"Whyever not? Surely it is clear that whoever committed this crime must have known how to negotiate the maze. What was to prevent one of them from entering after the game had begun?"

"That isn't possible," said Miss Pryce-Jones.

"Why do you say so?" demanded Holmes.

"About twenty years ago, there was a suspicion that the King and Queen had won by cheating – that they had come out of the maze, gone round to the front entrance and waited until they could slip forward and appear to have come through it. Nothing was ever proven, but since then a servant has been posted at the other four entrances to make sure that the players go in and do not come out again by any of them."

"That's one thing that wasn't in Kitson's *The Hedge Mazes of England*," I couldn't help remarking.

"It was written more than twenty years ago," retorted Holmes. He returned his attention to Miss Pryce-Jones. "Do you know of anyone else who would know the plan of the maze?"

Miss Pryce-Jones hesitated, then said, "Yes, there is one other person who would know. Margaret – Margaret FitzAlwyn."

"The daughter of the previous owner," Walcott informed us.

"Was she there on the night in question?"

"Yes, Mr. Holmes," said the young woman. "The Caerphillys broke a little with strict tradition by inviting her, as it meant there were forty-one guests instead of forty, but it was a courtesy to her, done out of kindness and consideration of the circumstances in which the FitzAlwyns had had to let go of the manor. Margaret's father had made some bad investments, and the family fortunes were in serious decline. Eventually, he came to the conclusion that the only way to pay off his debts and save the family from disgrace was to sell Elfrincham Manor. It was a terrible wrench, because the family connection to the Manor went back to the Thirteenth Century. Margaret was an only child, and she'd played in the maze when she was a little girl."

"By herself?"

"As far as I know. She did play with the village children, I think, but never with them in the maze. Her parents probably brought her up to respect its secret. So obviously, she didn't take part in the drawing of lots."

"Did she know Edward Crawley?"

Again, she hesitated.

"Yes, yes, she did," she replied, and drank the remainder of her glass of water.

"How well?"

"Mr. Holmes, Margaret FitzAlwyn is my friend. We were at school together . . . ."

"I'm afraid, Miss Pryce-Jones, that your duty to the truth must override your loyalty to your friend. I repeat: How well did she know him?"

"They were once engaged to be married."

"Since Edward Crawley has, or rather, had a wife, the engagement must have been broken."

"Margaret's parents had lived a very simple life after the sale of the manor. They managed to save enough for her to live fairly comfortably, and even take the occasional holiday now and then. It was on holiday, about six or seven months after her parents deaths, that she met Edward Crawley. Now it seems she'd never really had a beau, even though she was a perfectly presentable girl. She fell for Crawley totally, and there seemed to be every indication that he felt exactly the same toward her. Within a few weeks, they were engaged and planning to be married in late spring. By this time, she was living in a small apartment in London. Then one day, Margaret came down with a bad case of flu and was unable to go to a gallery opening in Bond Street that they'd both planned to attend. He offered to come over and sit at her bedside, but she insisted that he go along and enjoy himself.

"At the opening, he met one of the artists, Julia Bramwell. In many ways she seems to have been the polar opposite of Margaret

– confident, sophisticated, outgoing – and Crawley found himself falling in love with her almost immediately, and Julia returned the feeling. He really did try not to hurt Margaret, and struggled to control his passion, but in the end he couldn't stand it any longer, and three months before their scheduled wedding, he told Margaret that he couldn't marry her. Four months later he married Julia. Margaret was devastated. For about a year, she was walking around like a ghost, but then she recovered and entered society once more.

"Mr. Holmes, I can understand how you might suspect her of killing Edward, but I swear to you that that is impossible."

"How can you make that statement with such confidence?"

"I was sitting next to Margaret at one of the tables when the lots were drawn. She had complained of a headache and, just as I stood up to join Johnny and take my position at one of the entrances, she told me she was going back into the house to lie down in her room. I saw her walk away in the direction of the doors."

"Miss Pryce-Jones," said Holmes, rising, "I see no reason to detain you further. Thank you for your co-operation, and I wish you a safe and pleasant journey."

"I suppose," the young woman said a little bitterly, "that I am now Queen of the Maze, but as Juliet says, '*It is an honour I dream not of.*' Good day, gentlemen."

"Inspector Walcott, we have a few hours before sunset and, you may recall, I should like to examine the maze."

As the inspector had said, it was but a few minutes' drive to Elfrincham Manor. Holmes hefted one of the great brass knockers on the double doors and we were ushered into the drawing room and the presence of Lord and Lady Caerphilly by a tall, lugubrious butler.

"Good afternoon, my Lord, my lady," said Walcott with the characteristic deference of the policeman toward the aristocracy. "This is Mr. Sherlock Holmes and his colleague, Dr. Watson. I've asked them to help us out in this terrible business of the maze murder."

The Lord and Lady were in late middle age, both elegantly dressed in country clothes, and possessed of an amiable disposition.

"Holmes, eh?" said the Lord. "You're the fella who helped out the Conk-Singletons with that forgery business, right? * And that spot of trouble Backwater had a number of years ago."

"Correct, sir. Now, as we need to inspect the actual site of the murder, we shall need a guide to take us to the heart of the maze."

"Of course."

He rose from his chair and tugged at the bell-pull. The long-faced butler reappeared.

"Pearson, I believe Anderson is in the back orchard. Go and fetch him for us."

"Yes, my Lord."

"First rate fella, Anderson," the Lord continued when the butler had left. "Came with the house. Must have worked here for – Oh, what, thirty years?"

"I believe so, dear," said Lady Caerphilly.

"Ah, there you are, my good man," her husband said when Pearson reappeared a few minutes later with a short, sinewy man with iron-grey hair and a face as brown as a nut, dressed in plain work clothes. "Take these gentlemen to the centre of the maze."

"Right you are, sir."

The Elfrincham Maze was, indeed, an impressive sight. As Kitson's book had said, it was larger and more impressive than even its great counterpart in the grounds of Hampton Court. At seven feet in height, its green "walls" were taller than most men, and rising even higher was a ring of electric lamps on metal poles that served to illuminate it by night. The comparative gentleness of the curve that the front of the maze presented to us hinted at its great circumference. According to Kitson, its diameter was an impressive one-hundred-fifty yards.

"Were you here last night?" Holmes asked Anderson as we entered.

"That I was, sir," the gardener replied. "It was me as led the doctor to the centre of the maze. Horrible it was. Mr. Crawley lying there dead, blood all over his front, and that poor girl with a lump on the back of her head the size of a goose egg."

"What about before you took the doctor through? Were all the other maze gardeners there?"

"Oh yes, sir. All the servants were given the evening off. There was no one in the house. Me and the other mazers, we were at a table together, drinking from a barrel or two his Lordship had kindly given us."

I didn't take note of how long it took us to make our way through the maze, but I must confess that by the time we reached the centre, the narrow pathways threading backward and forward, the occasional unexpected curve and the towering green hedges were beginning to make me feel a little nauseous, and I was glad when we reached the open space. Holmes, as was his wont, seemed unaffected by the oddity of his surroundings.

"As I said, Mr. Holmes, no one has been here since poor Mr. Crawley's body was removed."

Holmes pressed a finger against his lips, silencing the policeman, and gestured to the three of us that we should remain where we were. For the next few minutes, he made a thorough examination of the space, at first stepping carefully, then going on his knees, and finally lying down full length. Eventually he stood and brushed down his clothes.

"Thank you, Anderson. I observed from the noticeboard at The Crown that dinner will be served at half-past seven. If you will take us to the local doctor now, Inspector Walcott, we should have ample time to question him and then get back to the hotel, to rest a little from our exertions and change for our meal."

The return journey through the maze was a little less onerous, but I hoped that our investigations wouldn't require us to enter there a second time.

It transpired that the surgery of Dr. Thomas Pocock was on a side-turning off the High Street, and thus only a few minutes' walk from The Crown. After giving us such simple directions as were necessary, Inspector Walcott departed for home with a promise that he would meet us the following morning after breakfast.

Dr. Pocock was a tall man in his late thirties with thick-lensed glasses, a full, neatly-trimmed beard, and a head of dark blond hair. His accent was, naturally, that of an educated man, but I fancied that I caught a hint of the familiar Sussex burr beneath his sophisticated tones, which suggested to me that he had returned to his home county to practice after he had completed his time at a teaching hospital.

He greeted us warmly.

"Inspector Walcott told me yesterday that I could expect a visit from you, gentlemen. I shall give you whatever assistance you need to find a solution to this ghastly business."

"If you could first tell us of the condition of Crawley's body as it was when you found it," said Holmes.

"I determined that the death had taken place about an hour or so before, The heart had been punctured several times by something long, thin, and pointed. Any one of these wounds would have been sufficient to bring about death by itself."

"And what of the Honourable Helena Broughton?"

"She was taken to the hospital in West Worthing. She was in a state of semi-consciousness, and from an examination of her head, I determined that she had probably been dealt a blow with a heavy blunt instrument at about the same time as Crawley was killed. I should say it will be a day or two before she can be questioned, and even then she may well be unable to remember any of the event."

I concurred.

"That is often the case in instances of concussion."

Holmes and I returned to the hotel and came down to dinner after a short rest in our separate rooms. The meal was doubly welcome. Neither of us had eaten since our breakfast in Baker Street that morning and, like the accommodation, it was of a higher standard than one would expect of such a rural establishment. Once the first course had taken the edge from my hunger, I was keen to hear what conclusions Holmes might have reached, but as there were several other diners present, he kept his own counsel, and our conversation was restricted to trivialities.

The hotel smoking room, however, was empty of fellow-guests, and as soon as we sat down to smoke our after-dinner cigars, Holmes spoke of the matter in hand.

"I learned little from the scene and, in truth, I didn't expect to glean much. Including Anderson and Dr. Pocock, no less than eight people had tramped all over it. What do you make of it thus far?"

"Well," I said tentatively after a pull at my cigar, "I agree that whoever the culprit is, he must know how to negotiate the maze. He managed to commit his crime and escape without encountering the other six people who were in there at the time. I think he must have gone into the maze before the contest began, and thus before the guards were placed. Is it not also possible that he remained in the maze until after Crawley's body and Helena Broughton were removed? The guards would be gone, and he could escape under cover of darkness."

"A credible scenario, but do you have any ideas as to the identity of the culprit?"

"We know that Margaret FitzAlwyn was present at the drawing of the lots, and also that she returned to the house, so we can eliminate her. The maze gardeners were all together at their table, but supposing an enemy of Crawley, whoever he was – "

"Yes," interjected Holmes. "If Mrs. Crawley is still at the castle, we should question her on that point."

"This enemy bribes one of the gardeners to reveal the secret, perhaps getting him to draw up a plan, and then, as I said, goes in before the contest begins and leaves after the victims have been found and taken out."

"Again, that is possible, although if Anderson is typical of the 'mazers', as he called them, it becomes less plausible. Such men as he usually place their loyalty to their masters above mere monetary gain, but it may be prudent to meet them all and see if we can assess their individual characters, And there are one or two other factors to be considered."

"Which are?"

"Even a single blow to the heart with such an instrument as Dr. Pocock described would produce a considerable amount of blood, would it not? More than had soaked into Crawley's shirt front – and there were several such blows. Yet there was no blood on the ground. That is one fact I did derive from my examination. The only other blood was on the front of Helena Broughton's dress, and it must have been Crawley's, because her wound was on the back of her head. Had it bled, we would expect the blood to be on the back of her dress. Does this suggest anything to you?"

"That Crawley's body was moved!"

"And the unconscious Miss Broughton must also have been moved, since the pair were walking the maze together. That might explain the blood on her dress. Now, to my second point: Dr. Pocock described the murder weapon as 'long, thin, and pointed'. What could that be?"

"A stiletto!"

"Watson, you scintillate this evening! But I think it unlikely that we would find an Italian instrument of assassination in a village in the Home Counties. A far more common object fits the description equally well: A hatpin. And while I would agree that it isn't wholly conclusive, it indicates that our killer may well have been a woman."

"Holmes! Supposing it was one of the other three women who went into the maze that evening? In fact, Victoria Pryce-Jones is a friend of Margaret FitzAlwyn. She may have hated Crawley for the emotional pain he had caused her, and killed him for that reason. She claimed to be going to America to visit relatives, but perhaps she has fled, never to return."

The detective gave a deep sigh.

"Ah, Watson! You were doing so well, but this theory flies in the face of the facts."

"Why? Margaret FitzAlwyn could have given her a plan of the maze, or they may even have gone into it together when they were friends at school."

"Perhaps, but that isn't the issue. Have you forgotten that the participants are chosen at random, by the picking of lots? It is beyond the bounds of probability that both the murderer and the intended victim would be picked, and even further beyond those bounds that the murderer's partner would be an accomplice to the crime, as he would have to be if the deed were to go unpunished. Remember that the players stayed in their pairs."

"Yes, of course. My apologies."

"Don't reproach yourself. Many would have done worse, and not all your ideas were without merit. Now, I am off to bed. We shall visit the manor house again tomorrow."

As he had promised, Walcott met us again the following morning with his dogcart, and we set out once more for Elfrincham Manor. *En route*, Holmes questioned the inspector about the "mazers" and received the following answer: "I've known all of them all the years I've been in the constabulary, and I'd vouch for the honesty and loyalty of all of them."

"None of them have been in any kind of financial difficulty?"

"When you're in their position, in this kind of area, you can't keep that sort of thing hidden, and I've never heard of any of them having anything of the kind."

"Could any of them had had any kind of grudge against Edward Grawley?"

"Well, Mr. Holmes, once the players have gone through the maze at Midsummer, they're never asked back. So every year there are at least eight new guests, and this year Mr. Crawley was one of 'em, so I don't think any of the 'mazers' even knew him."

At the manor, we briefly paid our respects to the Lord and Lady and inquired as to whether Crawley's widow was still in one of the guest rooms.

"Yes," replied Lord Caerphilly. "She's staying for the inquest, which is being held tomorrow afternoon, and then I understand the body will be taken to London for burial alongside his parents in Brompton Cemetery."

"And Margaret FitzAlwyn?"

"She was at breakfast. I believe she's still here."

We found Julia Crawley, *née* Bramwell, alone in her room, and in the course of a brief interview, she stated that her late husband had been well thought of by all who knew him and she was unaware of any enemies.

We returned to the Caerphilys' private apartments only to find them empty. Pearson the butler informed us that his master and mistress had gone out shooting with some of their guests and wouldn't be back for at least two hours.

"A pity," said Holmes. "I had hoped to act with their permission, but we cannot wait two hours. The solution to this mystery lies, I believe, below stairs."

"One of the servants?" asked Walcott, but Holmes didn't reply. Instead, he went back toward the main door and began to descend the stone steps to the kitchen, which were located near the bottom of the main staircase. Walcott and I exchanged puzzled glances, then followed him down.

In the kitchen, some of the servants, mostly female, were bustling about the room, busy preparing for the next meal. They stopped and turned their heads when we entered.

"Some of you know me," said the policeman. "I'm Inspector Walcott. "You may have heard of my friends here: Sherlock Holmes and Doctor Watson."

"You all know of the bad business in the maze," said Holmes. "We are helping Inspector Walcott with his investigation, and I need to ask you some questions. First, were all of you at the Midsummer celebrations?"

"None of us would miss that," said a matronly, middle-aged woman I took to be the cook. "One of the highlights of the year, that is."

There were nods of general agreement.

"We was all there – the kitchen staff, the mazers – yes, everybody. I don't recall anybody being missing."

"So, the manor house would have been completely empty."

"Well, yes."

"My second question: Has anything gone missing from here since the celebration?"

The cook spoke up again.

"Yes, one of the big food trolleys. But how did you know that?"

"My last question: What is the lowest point of the house?"

"That would be the cold room."

"Please direct us to it."

The cold room lay at the end of a corridor that sloped gently downward. Within, piles of various foodstuffs were neatly stacked against the right- and left-hand walls, but the back wall was clear. Holmes immediately went over to it, took his magnifying glass out, and began to examine the wall and the edges of the other walls where they met it. For two minutes we were all silent. Then Holmes gave a little cry of triumph, pressed one of the bricks on the left side, and stepped back. Before our eyes, the entire wall rotated through ninety degrees on a central pivot.

Holmes struck a match, and Walcott and I followed his light down a long stone corridor for about thirty yards until we reached a great circular hall supported by concrete pillars. At this point, Holmes's match died down. I reached into my own pocket for my box of vestas and struck one. By its light, we saw that as well as the pillars, there were four sets of spiraling stone steps that seemed to lead only to the ceiling. At the foot of one of them was what could only be the missing food trolley. Holmes climbed to the top, even as my match began to fizzle, and I saw him push upward with both hands. My vesta went out, but at the same moment a shaft of bright summer sunshine burst in upon us.

Walcott and I followed Holmes up the steps, and found ourselves in the centre of the Elfrincham Maze.

Holmes pushed back the block he had removed and pointed at it.

"I saw this when we were in the maze yesterday," he said, "but I didn't make the connection. It looks as if a tree has been cut down and its trunk levelled without being uprooted, but it conceals this secret entrance, and I have no doubt one would find something similar at the other three."

"I begin to see that in some way this was how the murder was carried out," said Walcott, "but who is the culprit?"

"And what is the purpose of that underground chamber?" I asked. "I can't believe it was built to facilitate murder."

"No, indeed. If I am correct, it was constructed for the preservation of human lives, rather than their destruction. The FitzAlwyns became High Church Protestants during the reign of Charles I, but before that, they were one of the richest and most prominent Catholic families in England. In the sixteenth century they were recusants, refusing to attend Church of England services and remaining loyal to the Pope and to the 'Old Religion'.

"For some time, '*recusant*' was just a label, but in 1593, Elizabeth I passed a statute which gave the term a legal definition and made recusancy a crime. There were four basic forms of punishment: Fines, confiscation of property, imprisonment, and execution. You were fined if it could only be proven that you weren't attending Church of England services, but if it could be shown that you had attended a clandestine Roman Catholic service, your property would be confiscated, and if you went on attending, you would be imprisoned or possibly executed. Rich families like the FitzAlwyns, who could afford to pay the fines, went on not attending C. of E. services, but were very careful not to be found attending Catholic services. Instead, they had their own priests to cater to their spiritual needs. If this was discovered, both the priest and at least the head of the family were likely to be executed. So the priests were lodged in secret chambers known as 'priest-holes'.

"There was a Jesuit priest called Nicholas Owen who specialised in designing and building them until he was executed in The Tower of London in 1606. In 1594, he was arrested and heavily fined. A wealthy Catholic family paid the fine and he was released. He then disappeared for three years until he rescued the Jesuit John Gerard from The Tower in 1597. Now, there's no record of which family paid his fine, but it's a reasonable assumption that it was the FitzAlwyns, and that a little later he embarked on a special project for them."

"1594 – that's the year the maze was planted," I interjected. "Are you saying he designed the maze?"

"No. I believe that at first the maze was nothing more than a blind, an explanation as to why there were so many people coming and going on the Elfrincham estate. I suspect that the reason why it's so large and complicated was so that it would take a long time and continue to be a cover for what was really being done – the construction of the underground chamber beneath it, which would provide a safe haven for not one but many priests. The stairs and concealed openings which give access to the maze were probably placed there so that if the chamber were discovered, the priests would stand a chance of escaping. They were doubtless informed how to negotiate the maze so that they could hide there until there was a possibility of escape, or until whatever danger there was, was over.

"When the FitzAlwyns became Protestants, the underground chamber became redundant and was eventually forgotten – until, that is, someone discovered it, presumably by accident."

"This is all very interesting, Mr. Holmes, but who is there for me to arrest?"

"Margaret FitzAlwyn. Here is how I read it, and how I reached that conclusion: She heard Edward's name called out as one of the maze walkers, and within a few moments had formulated a plan. From the order in which the names of the walkers were called out, she knew which entrance they would use to enter the maze, and therefore which paths they would be using until, as was likely, they reached the centre. So she went into the house, down into the cold room, through the secret door, and into the underground chamber. Using one of the concealed entrances, she went up into the maze and hid until she saw Crawley and Helena Broughton.

"I don't know what she hit Miss Broughton with, though I expect we shall find it if we examine the chamber. Crawley was probably too surprised to defend himself, and we know the first blow was fatal. That she went on stabbing him testifies to her hatred of him. Then she dragged them back down into the chamber. But how had she transported Crawley's corpse, and the unconscious Helena, to the concealed entrance nearest the centre? No woman would be strong enough to drag two dead weights through the chamber. That was why she took the food trolley. She must have put Crawley and Helena next to each other on the trolley, which, incidentally, explains the bloodstains on Helena's dress, and pushed them through the chamber until she reached the concealed entrance nearest the centre. Now she did have to drag them, but it wasn't too far. She likely took them up the steps one at a time."

"But," I remarked, "from what you have said, it couldn't have been premeditated. How did she know to have the trolley ready?"

"No, she didn't premeditate it, but she was thinking and acting quickly. All the servants were at the ceremony, so the house would be empty. She went straight down into the kitchen and took the trolley along the corridors, and down into the cold room and through the secret door. After she'd committed the crime, she went back upstairs and probably went to bed. And now, let us return to the underground chamber, since that will get us out of here more quickly than going through the maze."

Margaret FitzAlwyn was formally charged with the murder of Edward Crawley when her luggage was searched and found to contain the dress she had worn on that fateful evening. It was covered with bloodstains which she could not explain, and on being questioned by Inspector Walcott, she confessed. Her mental health was examined by a board of doctors, who determined that she should be placed in an institution rather than executed. As usual, Holmes allowed the police officer to take the credit for solving the case.

A few days later we read in *The Daily Telegraph* that Lord and Lady Caerphilly had decided that the Elfrincham Maze, and that singular underground chamber, should at last be open to the public. Holmes turned his attention back to his musical composition and produced a gentle air which, to this day, I still enjoy hearing him perform.

The Taverne Emerald

Mr. Sherlock Holmes, the consulting detective of 221b Baker Street, seldom took a holiday. He was wont to say, not without a little vanity, but also with some justification, that during his absence the London criminal classes would become more active, and take more liberties, than they would when he was in his proper place in the metropolis. Moreover, there was also the possibility that while he was away, crimes would be committed whose urgent solution was beyond the abilities of Scotland Yard.

Nevertheless, in the late summer of 189-, I accompanied him on a short cruise to Portugal, Spain, and the western Mediterranean. Why this was necessary, and what befell during that brief period at sea, I shall now relate.

The early months of that year were marked by repeated absences on Holmes's part. He did not neglect those cases which came to him in the usual manner, but took every opportunity to be off on some mysterious business of his own which kept him away from our lodgings for increasingly longer and more frequent periods.

My feelings regarding the situation were mixed. Whatever he was involved in, it was clearly absorbing his attention, making it less likely that he would experience that stifling *ennui* which, after all these years, might still lead him back to the use of cocaine. On the other hand, I was a little piqued by the fact that he hadn't chosen to take me into his confidence. I was no stranger to his habit of squirreling away some vital fact or deduction until the right dramatic moment presented itself, but this was the longest he had kept me in the dark – at least while we were occupying the same apartments.

One evening in April, alone in our rooms, I was looking up at the clock and wondering whether to have an early night or spend an hour or two reading the latest issue of *The Lancet*, when I heard Mrs. Hudson's voice raised in protest and the clump of heavy footfalls on the stairs. The door to our sitting room was then flung open and a sinister figure stood on the threshold. Clad in threadbare dark clothes, he was tall and bulky, but his back was somewhat bowed. He had a head of thick wavy red hair, a set of yellowed teeth, and a scar along the length of his left cheek. He came into the centre of the room with a shambling gait.

"Are you Holmes?" he asked in a distinct Irish accent.

"I am Dr. Watson," I replied, standing up from my chair. "Can I be of help?"

"Nah, it's Holmes I need to see. When will he be here?"

"I couldn't say."

"Now that's a pity, so it is."

So intimidating was the fellow's manner and aspect that my sight stole over to the nearest object I might use as a weapon – a fire iron standing next to the grate, a couple of feet from where I stood.

The fellow must have followed my glance, for he said:

"Sure now, there's no need for that. I've come here to help Holmes. Got some information for him. Patrick O'Flynn's the name."

"Mr. Holmes isn't here and, as I said, I have no idea when he'll be back."

"He's back now," the man said in a familiar tone, and piece by piece, the elements of the disguise – the red wig, the false scar, the padding used to bulk out his wiry frame – were removed, to reveal the face and form of my fellow-lodger. With a quick movement, he pulled a handkerchief from his pocket before doffing the shabby topcoat and then rubbed the yellow tincture from his teeth, and the transformation was complete. While my features no doubt registered my surprise, any comment I might have made regarding the imposture seemed superfluous, so I remained silent as Holmes reached for his Persian slipper and his old clay pipe and sat down with a sigh of pleasure. "Ah, the comforts of home! You are aware, of course," he said, filling the bowl, "that the late unlamented Professor Moriarty had two brothers, one a Colonel and the other a station master in the West Country."

"Of course," I replied, resuming my chair. "It was in response to Colonel Moriarty's letters in *The Times* that I felt compelled to set down the true story of our dealings with the Professor."

"Well, I received word from Shinwell Johnson that a Moriarty was attempting to revive his brother's criminal organization. I thought it unlikely that it was the station master, but I investigated him thoroughly to be on the safe side. He is actually a half-brother to the other two, some twenty years younger than the Professor and sixteen years younger than the Colonel. Since both of those gentlemen left home when he was still a young boy, it is unlikely that they had any malign influence on him. There is no evidence that he is other than what he seems, a law-abiding citizen with a responsible job who has remained in his immediate environs for some years."

"And the Colonel?"

"He served in India alongside Sebastian Moran, and it may well have been he who brought Moran to the Professor's attention. While he did nothing criminal on his return to England, he displayed two dangerous traits: He idolized his older brother, and, unlike the Professor, he is reckless and hot-tempered. Consider, for example, how injudicious those letters to *The Times* were. He should have realised that the investigation and the subsequent trials left no doubt as to the Professor's criminality."

"But you completely destroyed Moriarty's organization."

"Yes, I did, with, you must concede, more than a little assistance from Scotland Yard – and you, Watson."

"Then how can his brother revive it?"

"My dear Doctor, all of the criminals in London didn't belong to the organization. Parker, the garrotter, for example, did not, but upon my return he was very quickly recruited by Moran. And, sad to say, a fresh generation of criminals has arisen since our friend the Professor went over the Reichenbach Falls."

"What will you do, then?"

"I shall continue to gather information, both with Johnson's help and in my guise as Patrick O'Flynn, the cracksman from the Emerald Isle. The Colonel is, of course, nowhere near as gifted or as astute as his late brother, and so the whole affair provides none of the intellectual challenges presented by the older Moriarty. It is simply hard work. If I have kept my recent doings from you, it isn't out of secretiveness, but because they contained little of interest, and certainly not anything that you could spin into one of your compact little narratives."

"But why that particular disguise?"

"I considered it vital that I present myself as a complete outsider. Had I adopted the persona of a London criminal, there might have been those who were suspicious of the fact that I was unknown to them and had never been heard of in the metropolis. So I concocted a story in which I had fled Dublin in haste because the police were finally closing in on me. Hence the poor condition of my clothes. I also dropped fairly obvious hints that 'Patrick O'Flynn' might not be my real name, just in case anyone made enquiries in Ireland. You will recall that I keep several rooms around the city where I can change my appearance, and since the majority of the recruitment is taking place in the East End, it is to my foxhole in Aldgate that I have had most frequent recourse."

By the beginning of July, Holmes had accumulated enough evidence to prosecute Colonel Moriarty on several counts of criminal conspiracy, which also implicated the members of the higher echelons of his organization, to say nothing of being responsible for the arrest of many lesser felons, some of whom had been reckless enough to boast of their criminal exploits to "Patrick O'Flynn". But all this came at a great personal cost to Holmes. On the evening on which he informed me that his labours in this matter were now at an *end*, I called his attention to the physical toll the case had taken on him. He was pale-faced and more gaunt than ever. There were dark circles below his eyes, and, although he said nothing of it, I recognized the symptoms of someone suffering from occipital headaches and nervous spasmodic cramps.

"You have perhaps the strongest constitution of any man I have ever known," I began, "but there are limits to even your powers of endurance. I speak as both your friend and your medical advisor when I say that you must take a holiday. If you do not, there may be serious consequences – to your health, your sanity, and even your life."

"I am afraid you exaggerate, Watson."

"You don't trust my judgment, then, or my medical skill?"

"On the contrary. I have the highest regard for both – except where I am concerned."

"And what do you mean by that?" I said with some asperity.

"A husband should never treat a wife, a parent, a child, nor a friend a friend. Your connection to me compromises your diagnosis."

"I see. Well then, if you will not accept my opinion, will you consent to see a specialist? Penrose Fisher or Sir Jasper Meek? Or Charles MacNaughtan?"

Holmes agreed to see Meek. I accompanied him to the consultation, and though I was not, of course, privy to their conversation, I deduced from Holmes's unaccustomed air of contrition when he emerged from the surgery that the well-known expert had confirmed my conclusions.

And so it was that less than a week later we found ourselves in adjoining cabins on the *S.S. Amphitrite*, calling at Lisbon, Cadiz, Tangier, Gibraltar, Alicante, and Algiers. I had taken the precaution of booking us on board under assumed names, to prevent any problems that might arise from Holmes's celebrity. I embarked as Dr. James Wilson, while my friend was to be known as Simon Holland, thus ensuring that the initials on our luggage didn't betray us. Our only confidant was the captain, one Hamish Robertson, a strongly built man of middle height with a black, spade-shaped beard and a light Edinburgh accent.

On the first Saturday evening aboard the *Amphitrite* a dinner and dance was scheduled to take place in the ship's great hall. Holmes and I were invited to dine at the captain's table. There were ten of us in all, and when everyone was seated Captain Robertson, clad in an immaculate white dress uniform, made the introductions. On his immediate left were Emily Audley and her husband, Ronald Audley, Liberal M.P. for Ceredigion. Audley was known as a fast-rising member of his party, and expected to achieve high office when the Liberals returned to power. A tall, well-built man who held himself as upright as a guardsman, he exuded self-confidence, while his wife, the younger daughter of the celebrated society portraitist Edmund Lowery, seemed quite a frail creature. Her hair was mousy, her face pale, and her manner ill-at-ease. One had the impression that she couldn't easily keep up with her ambitious, energetic spouse.

Next to the Audleys was Lady Caroline Porter, a woman of unusual and striking beauty who was also an advocate of women's suffrage. Once known for the luxuriance of her chestnut hair, she now wore it in a short bob. She was outspoken in her views, and many young women were already adopting her distinctive style of dress, which was predicated on comfort and ease of movement rather than elegance. Sitting beside her was John Cardew, and beside him, opposite the captain, was Cardew's aunt, Lady Taverne.

The first thing that struck one about John Cardew was his remarkable good looks. He appeared to be as flawless as a Greek god: His hair was thick, black, and wavy. His skin was clear and without the slightest hint of a wrinkle, his eyebrows described two perfect narrow arches above his startlingly blue eyes, and below his straight nose, his regular teeth shone white behind his well-shaped lips. His manner was easy, and he spoke in an attractive light baritone.

Cardew's aunt, on the other hand, was remarkably plain. True, she must have been in her seventies, and thus well past the age by which most good looks have faded, but it was clear that even in her heyday she wouldn't have been pretty, let alone beautiful. Now her hair, well arranged though it might be, was clearly grey and wispy, her face and form almost painfully thin.

A complex net of wrinkles had gathered around her eyes, which were the same colour as her nephew's, but lacked any trace of their clarity and sparkle. And yet, whatever she looked like now, or had looked like in her youth, at least one man had seen beyond the transient, superficial envelope of flesh to the good, kind heart that lay beneath, and had loved her. Sadly, he had died early, leaving her alone and childless, and it was obvious to the most casual observer that she now lavished all her affection on her favourite nephew.

I was sitting on Lady Taverne's left, next to the Dowager Duchess of Swanley. The Duchess must have been widowed early, as she appeared to be in her mid-forties. She was short, trim, and blonde, and wearing a pale green dress discreetly decorated with pearls. Next came Holmes, and sitting between him and the captain was Isobel Dewey, an American heiress and a veritable Gibson Girl: Tall, green-eyed, and full bosomed, with her thick blonde hair piled high upon her head.

"Excuse me, Lady Taverne," said Ronald Audley when the waiter had finished serving us all aperitifs, "but is that the famous Taverne Emerald you're wearing?"

Everyone else at the table looked over at the old lady and the great stone in its elaborate silver filigree setting that hung from a chain about her neck. "Why yes, Mr. Audley."

"I'm a little surprised," said the M.P. "I rather thought you'd keep in a safe or a strongbox somewhere."

"Well, I hope you'll forgive an old woman's vanity, but I enjoy wearing it, and I like having everyone else see it. Besides,

I doubt very much if anyone here's going to try and steal it, if that's what you were thinking. And if they do," she concluded with a little laugh. "don't you know there's a curse on it?"

"A curse?" said the Duchess of Swanley.

"Yes."

"Oh, do tell us about it!"

Lady Taverne laid an affectionate hand upon the dark sleeve of her nephew's dress jacket.

"John can tell the story much better than I can. He knows all about it, don't you dear?"

"Is that all right with you, sir?" Cardew asked the captain.

"Oh, you go right ahead, laddie," said Robertson. "We've still got a few minutes before they serve dinner, and I'd like to hear the tale, too."

Cardew took out a silver case, lifted out a cigarette with an immaculately manicured finger and thumb, put it between his lips and, striking a vesta, applied the flame of the match to the end. He expelled a thin stream of smoke, blew out the match, and then, picking up his aperitif glass, he drained its contents and signalled to the waiter for a refill.

"Well then," he began, "according to the legend, there was a great temple in northern India, dedicated to the Hindu goddess, Parvati. On display in this temple, but closely guarded, was a small figurine of the goddess, carved from what was said to be the largest emerald ever mined in India at that point, sometime in the fourteenth century. For over two-hundred years, the statuette was safe. Then, in the middle of the sixteenth century, the temple was sacked by Pathan tribesmen who took the image as part of the loot."

"Ferocious warriors, the Pathans," I said. "I encountered them when I was serving in Afghanistan."

"Quite. Anyway, as Parvati's high priest lay dying from horrendous wounds, he put a curse on the Pathans and on any not of the Hindu faith who so much as touched the holy statue. The figurine was broken into four pieces."

"How did that happen?" asked Audley.

"That part isn't clear."

Cardew paused as the waiter refilled his glass.

"Thank you."

He took a sip of wine.

"As fanatical Muslims, the Pathans had no respect for anything the Hindus held sacred. Apart from despising what they saw as polytheism, they also believed that one shouldn't try to make pictures or statues of the divine. So perhaps they were simply destroying it as an image, or perhaps they were dividing it so that four deserving leaders could each have a piece. Whichever it was, those stones were eventually polished and recut and faceted so that no one might see the true nature of their origin, but the curse remained. The pieces went to four different destinations, and in time brought death and misfortune on whosoever had possession of them. I have to say, they must have passed through quite a few hands, but we only know about what happened to the famous ones."

He flicked the ash from his cigarette into the glass ashtray at the centre of the table.

"One found its way to the Ottoman emperor, Osman II, who was strangled at the age of eighteen in 1622 by one of his own Janissaries. It next turned up in Russia, where it is supposed to have caused the death of Czar Alexander II. Another piece was presented to the Mughal emperor, Dara Shukoh, who was assassinated by his younger brother Aurangzeb in 1659. The third piece wound up in Ethiopia. It fell into the hands of the Emperor Iyasu, who was murdered in 1706 at the order of his own son, Tekle Haymanot, who was apparently known as *Irgum*, which means '*the accursed*'. He outlived his father by less than two years, because he himself was killed by a rebel group of courtiers. What happened to those three pieces after that, no one seems to know."

"You see?" Lady Taverne said proudly. "He knows all about it. He even remembers the dates."

"As to the fourth piece," Cardew continued, "well, if you believe the story, that's what my aunt is wearing around her neck. Somehow, it reached England, where it caused the deposition and execution of Charles I. After the Restoration, James II inherited it and he was deposed too, in the Glorious Revolution, though he managed to escape to France."

"So how did it come to be in your family?" asked Lady Caroline.

"Lord Taverne's ancestor was a devout Catholic, and one of James's most ardent followers. The stone was given to him in recognition of his devotion to the King's cause, and ever since then it's been known as the Taverne Emerald."

"You're very quiet, Mr. Holland," observed Lady Caroline.

"I've never had much time for such fairy tales," said Holmes. "There are much better explanations for murder and assassination. Greed and ambition are more common, and likelier, than curses."

"Ah," said the captain, dispelling the momentary mood induced by Holmes's somewhat dour pronouncement, "here comes the first course."

All discussion of the jewel was suspended while we all turned our attention to the Brown Windsor soup. This was followed by fried Dover sole, accompanied by boiled new potatoes, garden peas, and tomato compote. The meal concluded with chocolate mousse and fresh fruit salad. All was washed down with a couple of bottles of Muscadet from the captain's own stock. When everyone had finished eating, another bottle was brought. Lady Caroline was the only smoker amongst the women. She produced a small bag of tobacco and a packet of papers, rolled a cigarette, and took a light from Audley, who then lit a Sullivan's for himself.

Holmes accepted a panatela from Captain Robertson and Cardew offered me a cigarette from his silver case. As plumes of smoke rose into the air, the table split into smaller conversational groups. The captain turned to Emily Audley, who was sitting on his left, and with his calm and reassuring air coaxed her a little out of the shy silence she had displayed for most of the meal. Next to her, the lady's husband was speaking across the table and applying his considerable charm to the Duchess of Swanley, who was smiling rather coquettishly amid little bursts of laughter.

I turned my attention to Lady Taverne and her nephew.

"Mr. Cardew – " I began.

"Oh, call me John, please."

"Well then, John, I wanted to ask you a little more about the Taverne Emerald, if you don't mind."

"Not at all. Please do."

"You said about the other three pieces that only the stories about the famous people who were affected by it have survived. But the Taverne Emerald – there must be more known about it, surely. Is there any more evidence for the curse?"

"You don't believe in it?"

"No, of course not. I'm just wondering if there any events in the Taverne history that might encourage others to. Any mysterious deaths, murders, anything of that sort? I like a good story, and this has me intrigued."

"The Tavernes have always been a military family, so one would expect a certain number of early deaths in the ranks. One of them, Ernest I think, was killed in the Crimea in 1854 in the Charge of the Light Brigade, at the age of twenty-six or so. Oh, and before that, a Taverne died in the Black Hole of Calcutta, 1756. Then there was the terrible scandal of 1867 – "

"Do you have to bring that up, John?"

"Come on, Aunt Jane, don't be squeamish. I'm just trying to answer Dr. Wilson's question."

"Oh, very well."

"Charlotte Taverne was the sister of the then-current title holder, and in possession of the emerald. She was swept off her feet by a dashing young officer in the Buffs called Reginald Tremayne. After a short engagement, they married and went to live in Canterbury, where the Buffs were garrisoned. But it seems the old adage, 'Marry in haste, repent at leisure', applies here, because it wasn't too long before Charlotte discovered that Tremayne was a wastrel, an utter cad. He gambled, and womanised, and quickly got through even the generous dowry the Tavernes had handed over. When Charlotte reproached him, he was violent towards her. She had to start wearing dresses with long sleeves and high collars, even in summer, to cover her bruises. She could only take this for so long. Finally the inevitable happened. She found someone else, an Italian music teacher. One evening Tremayne came home from a regimental dinner unexpectedly early and found them *in flagrante*. He took out a pocket pistol he always carried and shot them both. They died instantly. A maid who had heard the shots burst into the room and found Tremayne standing over the bodies with the gun still in his hand."

"Tragic," I said in a low voice.

"Well, yes," said Cardew. "Tragic enough, even though in some ways it's an old, old story. Charlotte's mother died not long after, and her brother, the fifteenth Lord Taverne, was a broken man for the rest of his days. I suppose some would attribute that to the curse. Oh, the orchestra's starting up! Excuse me – I promised the first dance to Miss Dewey."

The Audleys also got up and went onto the floor.

"Lady Taverne, would you care to dance with me?"

"Kind of you to ask, Captain Robertson, but my dancing days are long over. I'm sure the Duchess of Swanley would be pleased to accept your offer. And everyone – don't stay here on my account. Go off and enjoy yourselves."

"Are you sure you'll be all right on your own?" I asked.

"My dear boy, I'm used to being on my own. Now off you go."

Lady Caroline had stood and was waving to a friend at another table before going over to speak to her. Neither Holmes nor I had any taste for dancing, so we made our way over to the well-stocked bar just as the lights were being dimmed a little to provide a suitably romantic atmosphere.

"What do you make of John Cardew?" asked Holmes when we were both seated with a drink in hand.

"Well, he's a very handsome young man, well-mannered, and a fair storyteller."

"Ah, I should have known that that aspect of his personality would appeal to you."

"And he seems to be devoted to his aunt."

"She is unquestionably devoted to him, but I wonder how far that devotion is reciprocated. My suspicion is that he's taking advantage of her."

"You seem to know a lot about them."

"I know a little. She is in receipt of an allowance from her brother-in-law, which he isn't obliged to continue after he is married. And she can only use the title of Lady Taverne until then."

"Will she have to give up the emerald?"

"Yes, I believe so, and the probability is that he will marry soon. In the meantime, she appears to be lavishing most of her allowance on her nephew rather than herself. Her dress, for example, is quite old. It's been mended and redyed. Excellently done, but not well enough to fool a trained eye. You realize that Cardew has no blood connection to the Tavernes?"

"Really? He seems to know a lot about their family history."

"His mother was Lady Taverne's younger sister. She and her husband were killed in a train crash when Cardew was about thirteen. Lady Taverne was already a widow by then, and she took him in. When she dies, he'll be virtually penniless."

"What about Audley and his wife? They strike me as an ill-matched pair."

Holmes was about to reply when from the other side of the hall there arose an ear-piercing scream.

The orchestra fell silent.

"Oh my God! The curse of the emerald! Lady Taverne's dead!"

It was the Duchess of Swanley who spoke.

Then Captain Robertson cried, in a loud, commanding tone: "Please remain where you are, everyone. Stewards: Close the doors and windows. Lieutenant McAvoy, turn the lights up."

"Aye, aye, sir."

A tall young officer, clad in a similar white-dress uniform, left his table and hurried to comply with his captain's command. When the lights were up, Robertson went over to Lady Taverne and, kneeling down beside her where she lay, gave her a quick examination. Like all his officers, he had been trained in first aid.

"She isn't dead," he pronounced in a loud voice, and there was an immediate relaxation of the tension which had instantly pervaded the room.

"She seems to have fainted. McAvoy, fetch the nurse."

"Look! Look!"

It was the Duchess again.

"The Taverne Emerald! It's gone!"

"Everyone remain still. No cause for panic."

Robertson pushed Lady Taverne's chair, which had turned over, to one side and made a quick examination of the floor immediately around the fallen woman. There was no sign of the emerald. The only thing he found was her reticule, which he placed on the table. McAvoy returned with the nurse, who bent down and waved a small bottle of smelling salts under the old lady's nose. She came round quickly.

"It's gone! It's gone!" she cried in a shrill voice. The nurse, a brisk, efficient-looking woman in her early thirties, helped Lady Taverne to her feet, saying, in a lilting voice tinged with a Welsh accent, "Come with me, Lady Taverne. We'll keep you in the infirmary overnight, where we can take care of you. You've had a nasty shock. We'll see how you feel in the morning."

"Thank you," Lady Taverne said weakly, "but let me go to my cabin first. I want to get my nightdress, and some other things."

"All right, I'll take you there. How about that?"

"Don't forget this," said the captain, holding out the little purse. The old lady took it with a thin smile and then shuffled out of the room, the nurse's arm around her stooping shoulders, through a door held open by one of the stewards.

"I am afraid this isn't going to be very pleasant," the captain told us all. "The Taverne Emerald appears to have been stolen, and everyone will have to be thoroughly searched. Lieutenant McAvoy and I will search the gentlemen, and our two assistant nurses will deal with the ladies."

He looked over at another of the stewards.

"Tomlinson, fetch Miss Grierson and Mrs. Fitch."

"Aye, aye, sir."

Robertson came over to where Holmes and I were sitting and said, *sotto voce*, "It looks as if we may need your assistance, Mr. Holmes."

"Certainly not," I replied softly. "Mr. Holmes is on holiday, recovering from a long and exhausting investigation."

"I can speak for myself, Watson. Have everyone searched, and if there is no sign of the stone, I will give you what help I can. But on no account are you to reveal our identities."

I opened my mouth to protest, but then closed it without speaking. Holmes had set out his terms, and I knew from long experience that his resolve couldn't be shaken. The best I could do was to keep watch, and respond to any sign I might see that his health was endangered.

"I don't see John Cardew," said Holmes, looking around the room after the captain had gone about his business.

"Nor do I. Do you suspect him? After what you have told me, he seems a likely culprit."

Holmes glanced around once more.

"I don't see Isobel Dewey either. That settles it, I think."

In an hour or so, the long and somewhat embarrassing business of searching and being searched was concluded, without the emerald being discovered, and we were all permitted to go to our cabins for the night.

"Holmes," I said as we parted for our separate rooms, "you are still recuperating, and I am still your medical advisor. Don't stay up contemplating the solution to this case. Get a good night's sleep. Whoever the thief is, he or she cannot escape from a ship at sea. The mystery will still be there in the morning."

"As you wish. Goodnight, Watson."

When morning came, I was awakened by movement in my cabin, and opened my eyes to see Holmes standing before me.

"Good morning," I said, stretching a little. "You're up already."

My companion appeared to in a rather cheerier mood that he had been of late.

"I'm not just 'up'. I've already been for a little walk. You know – to stretch my legs, work up an appetite for breakfast, that sort of thing. And to confirm a suspicion I had. And would you credit it, I was right! Look!"

He reached into the pocket of his canvas jacket and pulled out a heavy object which dangled on the end of a silver chain. I jerked upright in bed.

"My God! The emerald! You've found it! The Taverne Emerald!"

"I didn't so much find it as steal it."

"Steal it? What are on earth do you mean?"

"Well, not last night. This morning. Technically it was theft, because I picked the lock and broke into the temporary dwelling of the person it belongs to, and took it from there without their knowledge or permission."

"The person it belongs to? You mean Lady Taverne? How could it possibly be in her cabin? It was stolen."

Holmes gave an enigmatic smile.

"Now, get up and get dressed, please, as we have something to do before breakfast, which is at eight. It is now a quarter-past-seven."

Five minutes later, we were strolling along the deserted decks under a brilliant, cloudless blue sky.

"You still haven't told me where we're going," I said.

"The infirmary, to speak to Lady Taverne."

"Are you sure that's wise? She had a terrible shock last night."

"Oh, don't trouble yourself on that account."

As we turned the corner to the infirmary, we found Captain Robertson waiting for us at the door, dressed in his dark blue peaked cap and working uniform.

"I got your note, Mr. Holmes," he said. "You'd better be right about this, is all I can say."

"If I'm not, then there will be a blot on my reputation, but no disgrace to the Attic Line, or to the captain of the *S.S. Amphitrite*. In any event, I've recovered the jewel, which is surely the most important thing. Shall we?"

The head nurse greeted us as we entered the hushed, slightly darkened rooms.

"Good morning, Mrs. Davies," said the captain. "We've come to see Lady Taverne. Is she awake?"

"Yes, sir, and she seems well enough to get up and have breakfast in the dining hall."

"Is anyone else here at the moment?" asked Holmes.

"No, sir."

"Good. Let us proceed."

Lady Taverne, who was sitting up in bed, looked rather surprised to see three people enter her room, but before she could speak, Captain Robertson said, "Excellent news, my Lady. The best possible. The jewel is recovered."

Holmes once more pulled the Taverne Emerald from his jacket pocket, but instead of the old lady's face suffusing with joy, it turned deathly pale.

"Lady Taverne," said the detective gently, "you would have made a fine actress, but a very poor criminal. I know you acted out of love, but having deduced your intentions, I'm afraid my conscience will not allow you to carry out your plan."

Lady Taverne broke into racking sobs. I instantly sat in the chair beside the bed and took her pulse. It was regular. Her hands were perhaps a little cold, which might well be attributable to her advanced age. At the same time, I doubted that she should be subjected to an interrogation, and shot a warning glance at Holmes.

He moved closer and said in a still gentler tone, "No true criminal would have tried to steal so conspicuous an object in such a crowded space, however dim the lights. Who is the only person who is never searched when such a crime takes place? The victim, of course. Your scream, your fainting fit, they were performed to make sure that everyone present was convinced that that was what you were. You were very lucky that no one saw you undo the clasp and slip the emerald into your reticule."

"How do you know that?" said Lady Taverne, the tears streaming down her wrinkled cheeks.

"Because that's where I found it when I went into your cabin, less than an hour ago. You insisted on returning there last night – not because you wanted to pick up your nightdress, but because you wanted to leave the reticule there, behind a locked door where there was no chance that its contents might somehow be revealed. And you did all this, you broke a lifetime's habit of honesty, all for your nephew, John."

"Yes, yes, for my lovely Johnny. When I die, he will have nothing. What could I do?"

"So the jewel was 'stolen' in front of a huge number of witnesses, and couldn't be found. You had it heavily insured, I think, and would put in your claim when you returned to England. In the meantime, you could sell the jewel at one of the ports we are calling at in the course of the cruise. There are plenty of places where no questions would be asked. The emerald could be broken up into smaller stones and those sold, and no one would be the wiser. That was it, wasn't it?"

"Yes, it was."

"Is John Cardew really worthy of such love as yours?" I asked.

"I know what he's like – what he is – if that's what you mean. Have you ever loved, Dr. Wilson?"

"Yes, yes I have."

"Then perhaps you will agree that if love was only given to those who are worthy of it, then very few of us would be loved. And now, could all three of you please leave me in peace?"

The cruise liner *S.S. Amphitrite* continued to make its leisurely way round the western Mediterranean, stopping at Tangier, Gibraltar, Alicante, and Algiers. The next Saturday there was a dinner and dance, and John Cardew danced each dance with Isobel Dewey. Lady Taverne had her meals brought to her cabin, which she never left for the rest of the cruise. As for Holmes, to my great relief he relaxed and seemed to enjoy the remainder of the holiday. One afternoon, we were standing at the ship's rail in the bright sunshine and gazing out over the blue-green ocean.

"There's one thing I don't understand," I began.

"What's that?"

"On the night of the 'theft', when you couldn't see either Cardew or Isobel Dewey, you said, 'That settles it.' What did it settle?"

"Well, like you, I at first considered Cardew the likeliest culprit. But he and Isobel Dewey were clearly taken with each other. I was sitting next to her, you may recall, and she never took her eyes from him. They had danced together, and then left the hall, no doubt for a little privacy. When, then, had he a chance to steal the emerald, even assuming he could somehow have lifted it from his aunt's neck without her knowledge? And however strong the attraction between them, Miss Dewey's complicity on such short acquaintance was unlikely."

A few weeks after the end of the cruise, Holmes and I were having breakfast in Baker Street when Mrs. Hudson came up with the morning papers. I selected *The Daily Telegraph* and, having already finished my boiled egg and toast, turned the pages, taking occasional sips from my cup of coffee.

"Dear me," I exclaimed.

"What's that?" asked Holmes, looking up from the Clarion.

"Lady Taverne's dead. Died in her sleep. They found her yesterday morning."

"It's on this page too," Holmes replied. "Births, marriages, and deaths. But listen to this: '*The engagement is announced today of Mr. John Cardew of 34 Tranmere Square, London S.W., to Miss Isobel Dewey of Baltimore, Maryland.'"*

"The American heiress. So 'lovely Johnny' has actually fallen on his feet . . . ."

"Quite so, but I haven't finished. '*On Saturday, 24th August, the marriage of Michael, Lord Taverne, to Gwendolyn Ruddick will be solemnized at St. Stephen's Chapel Westminster.'"*

"It's rare to find life being neater than fiction," I noted. "All the ends tied up in one day."

"Poor Lady Taverne. You know, sometimes I wonder if that curse isn't still at work, only in less obvious ways."

"Come, Holmes, you don't believe in curses any more than I do."

"A good woman very nearly became a bad one," observed Holmes. "A subtler horror than mere death."

"The key words in that sentence are 'very nearly'. That didn't happen, because you were there to stop it happening. And you wouldn't have been if I hadn't forced you into taking that cruise."

"*Touché*, Watson. No, it was love that created the situation. Love. The greatest curse of them all."

"For some. For others, the greatest blessing."

"As so often, old friend, we must agree to disagree."

Dinner at St. Luke's

My readers will perhaps recall that in 1895, Holmes and I visited one of our great university towns, where my friend carried out researches into early English charters. These researches were interrupted by the case which I have related in "The Three Students", but we were presented shortly after with another problem, the details of which I have refrained from making public. This was at the explicit request of Mr. Hilton Soames, who was still in a state of nervous agitation after the successful conclusion of the affair.

Despite the fact that Holmes's investigations entirely exonerated the College of St. Luke's and all its academic staff from any involvement in the death of Marcus Cullingford, lecturer in Ancient History, there was still gossip in the town concerning the nature of his demise. I assured Soames that if I chose to record either of the events which we had investigated, I would change the names of all those involved, and omit any details which would enable the reader to identify the college. He consented to my telling the tale of Gilchrist, McLaren and Daulat Ras, but baulked at the idea that I should turn Cullingford's death into a story for public consumption.

Now, however, many years have passed, and as I am maintaining the incognito of the college and its members, I feel that there is nothing to be achieved by suppressing the facts any longer.

Holmes returned to his researches in the university libraries on the day following the business of the unseen translation, while I took a morning walk through the town, had a pleasant lunch in a little pub by the river, and then returned to our lodgings to resume reading a yellow-backed novel I had brought with me.

At three o'clock there was a knock on my door, and I opened it to see before me the tall, spare figure of Hilton Soames.

"My dear Dr. Watson," he exclaimed with a smile. "It's all prepared. All settled. I have spoken to the other dons, and they are all agreed."

"One moment, sir. What is prepared? What is settled? And what have the dons agreed to?"

"That in consideration of the service you and Mr. Holmes have done the whole college in averting a scandal, we should like you to come to dinner at the High Table tomorrow evening. I assure you, our head cook is a virtuoso and the wines will be of the finest vintage."

"I will inform Mr. Holmes of your invitation."

"Splendid. We shall expect you at seven-thirty."

Holmes came back at a little after four, in a remarkably good mood. He strode into my room without knocking, a sheaf of notes clutched in one hand.

"I've done it, Watson!" he exclaimed. "I've established beyond question that the charter supposedly granting land to the

Bishopric of Athelney in 705 was in fact a forgery, made a hundred years later. Don't you see what that means?"

"I'm afraid I don't."

"Why, man, it means that all the rents and land taxes imposed by successive Bishops over the intervening centuries were essentially illegal. It makes the land common property. The Church may even have to reimburse the current tenants for the rents they've paid."

"That sounds as if it's going to have some serious consequences."

"Justice sometimes does, but it is justice, nevertheless."

He brandished the handful of papers.

"It's all here, and cannot be denied. I confess, Doctor, I feel like celebrating. A good meal and a bottle or two of fine wine, I think. What say you?"

The mention of food and drink reminded, me of the invitation to the High Table, so I informed Holmes of Soames" visit.

"You didn't accept?" he said with a groan. "You know how I feel about social gatherings of that kind."

"No, I merely said I would tell you that we had been invited. But I have to say, I think it would be churlish of you to refuse."

"Oh, you do?"

"Yes, Holmes, I do. You have done these fellows a great favour. Allow them to thank you in the best way they know how. If you don't, they will feel dishonoured."

Holmes gave a deep sigh.

"Very well. I suppose it is a small price to pay for the interesting little problem with which Soames presented us."

The following evening found us in St. Luke's dining hall at the designated hour. We were greeted effusively by the company and, when the first glasses of wine were poured, Hilton Soames led a toast in our honour. As he had promised, the food and the wine were both excellent. The first course was pea-and-ham soup, followed by crab flakes in a shrimp sauce with mayonnaise and Dijon mustard. The main part of the meal consisted of shoulder of mutton in gravy accompanied by boiled new potatoes, green beans, and broccoli. The dessert was hot apple pie with Devonshire clotted cream. All this was washed down with a fine Bordeaux.

I confess that I do not remember the names of those at table as well as I recall the repast. Whatever they might be like when encountered individually, collectively their demeanour had that combination of the schoolboy and the monk which frequently marks those men who have had no significant contact with women of their own class since leaving their mothers to go to one of the public schools. Their conversation consisted mainly of gossip about academics from the other colleges, little jokes at each others' expense, and observations related to their own individual disciplines. One man who did stand out, however, was Marcus Cullingford, and this was not solely because this was fated to be the last night of his life. To judge from the greetings he received when he took his seat – "Didn't expect to see you here, Cullingford" and "Finally decided to dine with us, eh?" and the like – I assumed that his presence at such gatherings was a rare event. Another thing which made him worthy of note was that he was the youngest of the company, with a full head of dark hair in contrast to the bald pates or white hair of the majority of the dons. He said little, but consumed rather more wine than the others.

Holmes had also remained largely silent throughout the meal, which he had clearly enjoyed, but was subject to a little ragging when brandy and cigars were served.

"University man, Holmes?"

"Yes, though not, I regret to say, at this estimable establishment."

"Detective, eh? Bit of a rum sort of profession, what? Sneaking around and digging out people's secrets."

"It provides me with my bread and cheese and, as Watson here can tell you, once or twice we've been able to serve our country by 'sneaking around and digging out people's secrets'."

"Is that so?"

"Please remember that Mr. Holmes and Dr. Watson are our guests of honour," interjected Hilton Soames.

"Perhaps you could tell us a little about some of your other exploits," suggested another of the dons.

"Ah, storytelling is Watson's department," said Holmes.

I then regaled the company with the case of the Bogus Laundry, which had the advantages of being relatively short and easy to relate, while demonstrating both Holmes's powers and his patriotism.

"You didn't do much in that, Watson," observed Cullingford, who was now beginning to look somewhat inebriated.

"My friend is a modest fellow," said Holmes, "and he continually underplays those personal characteristics which make him the perfect companion and helpmeet. And in a dangerous situation, there is no one I would rather have at my side."

"That's told you, Cullers!" chuckled a short, tubby don whose head was completely bald, apart from a circle of fluffy white hair at the back.

Cullingford did not reply, but gave the man a venomous look which seemed wildly out of proportion in response to that mild piece of badinage.

Holmes and I returned to our lodgings at about eleven o'clock.

"Admit it, Holmes," I said as we climbed the stairs. "You enjoyed the meal."

"Yes."

"Even if the company was a little lacking."

"The most interesting one was Cullingford. There's something eating away at that man, though as it is unlikely to be criminal, it does not come within our purview."

His words proved slightly prophetic, for an hour or so after we had our breakfast the following morning, there was a frantic knocking at the door of our lodgings. The landlady opened it to reveal the presence of Hilton Soames, who looked straight past her to Holmes, just coming into the hall, and about to head off for another day's research at the university library.

"Mr. Holmes! Mr. Holmes! You've got to help us!"

His voice was high with anxiety and a cold sweat was forming on his pale, broad forehead.

"Good Heavens, man! What is it?"

By this time I had heard the commotion and came to see what it portended.

"It's Marcus Cullingford! He's been murdered!"

"Murdered? How?"

"Has the university doctor been consulted?" I asked.

"Yes, and he thinks it's poison, though without an autopsy he can't say what kind."

"The police will have to be called in," said Holmes.

"That's why I'm here. I want you to take a look at him. Perhaps you can sort this out without informing them."

Holmes gave the agitated academic a stern gaze.

"We will, as you say, take a look at him, but the police will have to be told eventually. And if we come to the conclusion that someone who was at table with him, or one of the catering staff, was responsible, we will not withhold that information from the constabulary. Is that understood?"

"Yes, yes. I have a cab waiting."

As we were driven through the historic mediaeval streets, Holmes asked, "Did the university doctor decide on a time of death?"

"Some time in between two and three this morning, he said," replied Soames.

"That might well suggest that the poison was administered during the dinner. Who discovered the body?"

"Cullingford's scout. He came into the bedroom to wake him, as usual, at about 8:30. It was obvious from the terrible expression on his face that he was dead, and had died in agony. The scout came to fetch me, and I went to summon Dr. Cartwright."

"Did Cartwright carry out the examination *in situ*?"

"Yes. Nothing has been moved, as I decided to ask you in almost immediately."

Soames hesitated.

"Before we reach Cullingford's rooms, there is something I must tell you. You must have gleaned from some of the remarks made when he sat down that Cullingford had not attended the dinners in some time. I learned from Dr. Cartwright that Cullingford came to him some time ago suffering from stomach cramps. He believed that someone was slowly poisoning him, but the doctor assured him that the cramps were caused by overwork and nervous tension. Cullingford apparently did not take the medication Cartwright prescribed in case it was the doctor who was trying to kill him. This obsession grew until Cullingford ate all his meals in town and refused to socialize with the other dons. But now . . . ."

"You think his suspicions may have been justified."

"Yes."

"Did he have any enemies?"

"Dons have rivalries, not enemies – at least, that is usually the case. I can't think of anyone who disliked him enough to murder him."

We arrived at an ivy-covered court very similar to the one occupied by Soames, which was arranged on virtually the same pattern. Cullingford's rooms were on the ground floor. A porter admitted us, and Holmes turned to Soames.

"We will come to your office as soon as we have anything to report."

"Thank you."

As the don hurried across the court, I remarked, "You were rather harsh with him."

"I only agreed to this because Soames was obviously distressed. There is little we can do here. The police must know, and soon. A lengthy investigation will probably ensue, and we have no time for that. We are due to return to Baker Street tomorrow."

We entered Cullingford's suite of rooms. The late lecturer in Ancient History lay on his back in bed, and his mouth contorted into a truly horrific rictus. Dr. Cartwright had not closed the dead man's eyes, and their pupils had rolled upwards to the limit of their orbit. I concurred with the university doctor's diagnosis that poison was the probable cause of death.

"Let us see if the other room can afford us any useful data," said Holmes. That room was dominated by books and papers, the shelves being crowded almost to the point of collapse with teetering towers comprised of further volumes in front of them. There were two piles of essay papers, presumably marked and unmarked. There was also a locked cupboard, but Holmes drew my attention to an escritoire in the corner of the room which was entirely free of clutter, there being only one sheet of paper on it.

"Presumably this paper was of some importance, since Cullingford appears to have made a point of keeping it separate, so that it would be to hand when needed. Let us see what is on it."

He looked at it for about half a minute. Then, handing the paper to me, said, "How's your Latin, Watson?"

"A little rusty."

I read:

Nobilissimum autem est Mithridatis, quod cottidie sumendo rex ille dicitur adversus venenorum pericula tutum corpus suum reddidisse. In quo haec sunt: costi P 1.66acroi P.V 20; hyperici, cummi, sagapeni, acaciae suci, iridis Illyricae, cardamomi, singulorum P.8 II; anesi P.12 III; nardi Gallici, gentianae eradj, aridorum rosae foliorum, singulorum P.16 IIII; papaveris lacrimae, petroselini, singulorum P.17 IIII casiae, silis, lolii, piperis longi, singulorum 20. 66 V styracis P.21 V castorei, turis hypocistidis suci, murrae, opopanacis, floris iunci rotundi, resinae terebenthinae, galbani, dauci Cretici seminis, singulorum P.24.66 VI nardi, opobalsami,

singulorum P.25 VI thlaspis P.25 VI radicis Ponticae
P.28 VII; croci, zingiberis,cinnamomi, singulorum
P.29 VII Haec contrita melle excipiuntur, et adversus
venenum, quod magnitudinem nucis Graecae impleat,
ex vino datur. In ceteris autem adfectibus corporis pro
modo eorum vel quod Aegyptiae fabae vel quod ervi
magnitudinem impleat, satis est.

I endeavoured to translate what I could.

"*Rosae foliorum* – rose leaves. *Cardamomi* and *cinnamoni* are almost the same in English. *Anesi* is anise, *terebenthinae* is turpentine, and *zingiberis* is ginger, and *croci i*s saffron. Is this some sort of recipe?"

"In a way, yes. I believe this lists the ingredients of a *mitridate*, named after an ancient king of Pontus, who is mentioned in the first line. Have you heard of it?"

"As a doctor, of course I have. It is a concoction supposed to act as a universal antidote against any form of poison. But surely, it's entirely mythical."

"Well, whoever wrote this clearly didn't believe so, and neither did Cullingford. As a professor of ancient history, he would have heard of Mithridates, who wished to avoid the fate of his father, who was assassinated when Mithradates was twelve. According to one version, he took different kinds of poisons in small doses to build up immunity against them, but others say he developed this universal antidote, and after his death at a ripe old age there were several attempts to recreate it, of which this, I fancy, is one – probably from Celsus' *De Medicina*. Some of the ingredients here would have been very difficult and expensive to get in those days, so its efficacy probably wasn't often put to the test, but there would be little difficulty obtaining them now. Do you begin to see how this explains Cullingford's behaviour?"

"He didn't attend the meals because he thought someone was trying to poison him, but he put the mitridate together and took it before the dinner. Believing himself immune, he ate and drank freely. But the mitridate didn't work, and he succumbed to whatever poison was administered to him."

"Possibly," said Holmes, "but I believe there is a simpler answer, and if I am not mistaken, the answer may be found in this locked cupboard. Fortunately, it is my reprehensible habit to carry my lock picks wherever I go."

He worked at the doors for a few seconds, then threw them open. Inside were three shelves, on which stood a number of large bottles of the type found in chemists' shops.

"The ingredients, I believe. In large amounts, because the effect of each individual dose would not be permanent – assuming one believes it would work at all."

"Did he eat all those things?"

"No. According to the paper they have to be dried and then ground, so there's probably a mortar and pestle here somewhere. Yes, here at the back. So they were dried and ground and mixed with honey, then formed into a pellet which was swallowed."

Holmes unscrewed the lids and examined the contents one by one, until, on opening the seventh, he gave a small "Ah!" of satisfaction.

"You have found the answer?"

"Yes. Let us go and inform friend Soames of the news."

"Come!" yelled Soames in answer to Holmes's knock.

"Good news, Mr. Soames," said Holmes. "You may safely report this matter to the police without an ensuing scandal or investigation. Marcus Cullingford was the author of his own demise, as the police autopsy will confirm."

"Suicide?"

"No, no. An accident, the unfortunate result of a misinterpretation of a Latin text. Mr. Cullingford must have been slightly less proficient at Latin than he imagined, and he certainly had no knowledge of toxicology."

"Please explain."

Holmes gave Soames a brief description of what we had found, and the significance of the paper bearing the Latin text, which he had brought with him.

"The formula contains rhubarb. Cullingford must have interpreted this to mean rhubarb *leaves*, of which he had a large supply, rather than rhubarb *stalks*. Now, while rhubarb stalks are harmless, the leaves contain a high concentration of oxalic acid, which can cause failure of some of the vital organs. Drying and grinding them probably concentrated it further.

"Normally that would produce great pain, so I can only surmise that one or more of the other ingredients in the mithridate acted as an analgesic while it did its work, enabling him to attend the dinner with no signs of the ill effects. No doubt the autopsy will also reveal the truth of that."

"Thank you, thank you, Mr. Holmes. And you, Dr. Watson."

"You're welcome, Mr. Soames. And now, Watson – Baker Street calls."

The Adventure of
James Edward Phillimore

It had been raining heavily in London for more than a week. One morning after another, I awoke in semi-darkness with a chill in the air and water streaming down the panes. It was a pleasure, then, to rise from sleep that day in late April to see and feel the sun beaming through the windows of my bedroom in Baker Street. I had no doubt that the cessation of the daily downpours would also be welcome to my fellow-lodger, Mr. Sherlock Holmes. He was largely indifferent to the weather except when it affected his practice as London's first and only consulting detective, and, as he had remarked to me on more than one occasion, clients were less likely to call, and criminals to carry out their misdeeds, when there was heavy rain.

I shaved and dressed with a light heart and descended the stairs, eager to see what Mrs. Hudson had provided for our breakfast. When I entered our sitting room, I found Holmes already half-way through a plate of kedgeree, a dish for which I had acquired quite a taste during my time in India.

"Good morning, Watson," he said with a wide smile. "A pleasant morning, is it not? Perhaps when you have consumed Mrs. Hudson's excellent meal, you might like to come for a walk with me in this spring sunshine."

"By all means," I answered as I spooned a portion onto my plate.

I haven't spoken much in these chronicles of the frequent excursions that Holmes and I made from our lodgings into the wider world of the metropolis. He often claimed that he allowed his brain to retain nothing other than that which was strictly necessary to the pursuit of his profession, but in his more relaxed moments he was prepared to concede that this wasn't strictly true. A thorough knowledge of the layout of the city was, naturally, of great practical use to the detective, but this could not be said of the majority of the out-of-the-way facts he had accumulated over the years. Wherever we went, it seemed, he had an anecdote about the district's past inhabitants or the story of the origin of the name of a particular road or area.

When we had finished our coffee, and Holmes had smoked his first, malodorous pipe of the day, we went down into Baker Street and set off at a leisurely pace in a north-easterly direction.

After a pleasant stroll into lower Islington, during which Holmes informed me that the name of the borough had originally been "Giseldone", meaning "Gisla's Hill", after an early Saxon inhabitant, we returned to Baker Street some two hours later. On our entry, Mrs. Hudson handed Holmes a visiting card and informed us that a lady had called in our absence – young, about twenty-two or -three, and well-to-do.

We climbed the stairs to the sitting room and when I had sat in my accustomed armchair Holmes passed me the card, saying, "Let me hear what you can deduce from this."

On the printed side it said: *James and Viola Phillimore, The Poplars, 17 Oulton Rd, Bromley, Kent.*

I turned it over. On the other side was written, in a neat, feminine hand: *Will call again at half-past eleven. VP*.

"Well," I began, a little hesitantly, "the Phillimores are evidently well-off. The card is particularly thick and stiff, and the information is embossed, rather than merely printed on it."

"A reasonable inference."

"While it is clearly expensive, it is not ostentatious, which indicates modesty and good taste on their part."

"Sound enough. Anything more?"

"Not to my eyes."

"It isn't your eyes that are at fault, since they see no less than mine. You fail to deduce from what you see."

I passed the card back to him, sighed, and reached in my pocket for my pipe and tobacco pouch, saying as I filled the bowl with Ship's, "What do you deduce then?"

"We already know from Mrs. Hudson that Viola Phillimore is a young woman. I would add that she and her husband have probably not been married long, are childless, and have only recently moved into The Poplars, which is in all probability their first marital home. Mrs. Phillimore is a sensible woman, not given to hysteria, so we may take it her visit to us has a serious purpose."

He handed me back the card.

"Observe," he continued. "Despite its stiffness, the card is slightly bent, and there are two small indentations on the lower edge."

"Why, yes. And what does that tell us?"

"That too many cards have been pressed into a card case. Which also tells us that the carrier of the case anticipated handing out many cards on the day the case was filled. When would one hand out more cards than at any other time? When one has just moved into an area and is calling on one's new neighbours."

"Very well, but your other deductions? Their childlessness, and the rest?"

"Both of the couple's names are on it. If the husband is, as we may infer from their address and the quality of the card, a member of the professional class, he doubtless has his own supply of cards with only his name upon them. His wife doesn't have her own cards, which indicates that she does not yet move comfortably in her new social circle unless accompanied by her husband. That is a characteristic of the early days of a marriage, especially among younger women. It is also her youth which persuades me that she has no children. It is among the lower orders, to which she clearly doesn't belong, that we must expect to see early marriage and young parenthood."

"How do you arrive at your conclusions about her personality?"

"Really, Watson! We have a sample of her handwriting, brief though it is! Women tend to write in a smaller hand than men and, allowing for that, her writing is of the middle size, which generally indicates a well-balanced personality. This inference is corroborated by the neatness of her script and the fact that the letters of her words are consistently connected."

"Well," I glanced up at the clock where it sat on the mantelpiece next to Holmes's jack-knife, "we don't have long to wait before we can test the accuracy of your conclusions."

Mrs. Viola Phillimore was a handsome young woman of the middle height, dressed in a modest outfit of dark blue taffeta, and with a small dark hat pinned to her hair, which was a deep chestnut in colour. Distress was visible on her pale, heart-shaped face.

"Good morning, Mrs. Phillimore. I am Sherlock Holmes, and this is my colleague, Dr. John Watson."

"Dr. Watson. I have, of course, heard your name in connection with that of your friend."

"Please take a seat, Mrs. Phillimore," said Holmes, "and tell us how we may be of service."

"Certainly, Mr. Holmes. My husband is James Edward Phillimore, a junior partner at the solicitors' firm of Killroy and Hay in the City, and we have recently moved into The Poplars, in the southern part of Bromley in Kent. Four days ago, on Saturday, we had just left the house at about half-past eight to visit my mother in Norwood, and were about to walk to the station when James realized that he had left his umbrella in the stand in the hall.

"'I'd better go and get it,' he said. 'It'll rain today, if the last few days are anything to go by. I'll just be a moment.'

"He turned his key in the lock once more and went in, closing the door behind him.

123

"Getting the umbrella should have been the work of a few seconds, so when a couple of minutes had gone by without his return, I took out my own key and opened the door, which had automatically relocked when James re-entered. The umbrella was still in the stand, but James was nowhere to be seen. I thought perhaps that he had forgotten something else, from another part of the house. I called out his name once or twice, but there was no reply. I went back to the door and looked down the street in either direction, but still he was nowhere to be seen. I stood for a while, dazed and baffled, then I went to the local police station to report his disappearance."

"Where, I would imagine, they were less than sympathetic," said Holmes.

"They seemed to think that either he was playing some absurd prank on me, or that he wanted to leave me and had chosen this particularly cruel method of doing so. They told me to wait a few days for his return. I have done so, with no result, so now I have come to you, Mr. Holmes."

The detective leaned forward, resting his elbows on his bony knees and pressing the tips of his fingers together.

"Before I take your case, let me warn you that should I discover the truth, it may not necessarily end your distress."

"I understand that, Mr. Holmes. Nevertheless, I wish to know it."

"Very well. Now, if you would be so good, I have some questions to ask you. Were there any servants in the house on that day?"

"No. We have a cook, and a maid, but neither of them lives in, and as we visit my mother every Saturday, we give them that morning and afternoon off."

"You said that you looked up and down the street without seeing your husband. Did you see anyone else?"

"It was quite early in the morning, and a Saturday. The street was empty except for a deformed man I had never seen before, about thirty yards from the front door. As I looked at him he turned and hobbled away. Since my husband has a straight back and a strong physique, it couldn't have been him, even if for some outrageous reason he had been disguised."

"Have you made inquiries at Killroy and Hay?"

"I have just returned from there. When I didn't find you in, I decided to use the time to call on them."

"And?"

"He hasn't been at their offices since last Friday."

"Now I must ask you some questions of a more delicate nature."

"Please proceed."

"How were the relations between your husband and yourself?"

"No marriage is ever perfect, Mr. Holmes, or utterly without conflict, but I believe that ours was as harmonious as one could reasonably expect. I am certainly happy, and James gives no indication that he is not."

"You have never had any doubts as to his fidelity?"

"Certainly not. James is a quiet man. He seldom goes out without me, and while he sometimes stays late at his chambers, he often brings any extra work home. I cannot see when he would have the time to be unfaithful, even if he had the inclination, which I can assure you he does not."

"Has there been any change in his habits of late?"

" He had been spending rather more time in his study over the last few days before his disappearance, but I gather that he has several important cases on at the moment."

"I see," said Holmes, standing up. "Dr. Watson and I will need to see your house. May we do that this afternoon?"

"Yes, of course."

"Then we bid you goodbye until then, Mrs. Phillimore."

After Mrs. Hudson had shown the lady out, Holmes asked, "So, my friend, what did you make of her story?"

"Well, people don't simply vanish into thin air."

"Don't they, now? What about Bathurst?"

"No doubt I am very slow, Holmes, but I fail to see what Australia has to do with this."

"I was referring to Benjamin Bathurst, not the gold centre of New South Wales. On 25 November, 1809, Bathurst, a British diplomatic envoy, and his German courier, a Herr Krause, travelled by chaise to the town of Perleberg, west of Berlin. After ordering fresh horses at the post house, Bathurst and his companion walked to a nearby inn, The White Swan. They ate an early dinner, and then Bathurst spent several hours writing in a small room set aside for him at the inn. The travellers' departure was delayed and it wasn't until nine p.m. that they were told that the horses were about to be harnessed to their carriage. Bathurst immediately left his room, followed seconds later by Krause. Bathurst entered the chaise, but when Krause went in, he found it empty. He went around the horses to see if, for some reason, Bathurst had stepped out through the other door. But there was no sign of him anywhere."

"So what had happened?"

"No one knows. That's my point. Perhaps I am being a little vain in thinking that had I been in Perleberg at the time, I would have solved the conundrum. In this instance, I'm rather afraid that Mr. Phillimore, as the Bromley constabulary suggested, has left his wife, though at present I am at a loss to explain why he should have done so in such a bizarre manner. However, let us not speculate further until we have more data."

After a light lunch, we made our way to Liverpool Street and caught the two o'clock train to Bromley South. From there it was a short walk to Oulton Road. Mrs. Phillimore greeted us with a countenance suffused with hope. I had expected Holmes to make a thorough search of The Poplars, but instead he asked, "Is there any part of the house to which only your husband has access?"

"Yes, there is his study. He doesn't even allow the maid into it, which I grant is a little eccentric, but as I told you in Baker Street, he sometimes brings work home, and if he needs absolute privacy to concentrate on it, then so be it."

"May we see it?"

"I'm afraid that my husband has the only key, which he keeps on a ring that only he handles. It will have been in his pocket when he . . . when he . . . ."

Mrs. Phillimore's calm demeanour broke down and she burst into passionate sobbing. In that moment, she seemed like a desperate young girl rather than the composed married woman we had first met that morning. Clearly this business was putting her under considerable strain

"Put your faith in Mr. Holmes," I said soothingly. "If this mystery is capable of solution, then he is the man to solve it."

"And if we are to solve it," said Holmes, "then I am afraid that, with your permission of course, I must pick the lock of Mr. Phillimore's study."

"You have it," said Mrs. Phillimore, "but you will forgive me if I don't watch you at your work. I shall be in the parlour."

Once the lady had gone, Holmes took a little soft leather case from the pocket of his jacket and selected two metal tools from it.

"This will take but a moment. The lock isn't a sophisticated one." And within an instant, the door was open, and we stepped into James Edward Phillimore's private sanctum.

It was a square, spacious room with one small window, unremarkable at first glance except for a deal table covered with jars of chemicals and scientific equipment. It seemed that, like Holmes himself, Phillimore was an amateur chemist. The detective looked at the jars one by one, then turned to an examination of the rest of the room. Its walls were covered with a plain, conventional wallpaper, another indication of that modesty and lack of ostentation hinted at by the visiting card. The dark blue, unpatterned carpet, the brown mahogany desk, the white lampshade, the utilitarian furniture, all pointed to an occupant of simple, unaffected tastes.

On the wall behind the desk were two framed photographs, one of the couple together, clearly taken on their wedding day, and the other of Mrs. Phillimore by herself. Between the photographs was a set of shelves bending slightly under the weight of the books upon them.

"What a man chooses to read is among the best indicators of his character," said Holmes, and we began to scan their spines. As might be expected, given Phillimore's profession, there were many books on the law, but they were all crammed onto the top shelf. Those below were of more interest and, to judge from their condition, more frequently read:

The Zincali, *Lavengro*, and *The Romany Rye* by George Borrow, *Travels with a Donkey in the Cevennes* by R. L. Stevenson, *Confessions of an English Opium-Eater* by Thomas de Quincey, *The Gold Mines of Midian* and *The Lands of Cazembe* by Sir Richard Burton, *Tales of the Grotesque and Arabesque* by Edgar Allan Poe, and two volumes *of La Comedie Humaine* by Honore de Balzac.

"Are you beginning to discern a theme?"

"Travel. Escape."

"Certainly, but I think we can infer a little more. Let us consider the authors for a moment, rather than the content of their works. Stevenson rebelled against his Presbyterian background and the path laid out for him by his father. Borrow and Balzac both studied law, but found it stultifying, and rejected it in favour of literature. Poe was always at odds with his foster-father and failed at the military career planned for him. When Burton was at college, he deliberately tried to get rusticated by breaking every possible rule. De Quincey was sent to Manchester Grammar School, so that after three years' stay he might obtain a scholarship to Brasenose College, Oxford, but he ran away after only nineteen months."

"All rebels, " I said. "Defying what was expected of them."

"Indeed, and unless I am very much mistaken, if we look into Phillimore's background we shall probably find indications that he wished for a different life, but hadn't the strength of character to go against his family's expectations."

"Holmes, both de Quincey and Poe were opium eaters. Do you think Phillimore emulated them?"

"One thing is clear: While part of him longed to escape from the prison of respectable conformity, he remained within it because he loves his wife. Here, in his private space, where no one else would ever see them, he has a wedding photograph and a portrait of her."

"What now?"

"A visit to Messrs Killroy and Hay, I think. But first, a word with Mrs. Phillimore."

Holmes locked the door once more with the aid of his metal picks and we made our way to the parlour.

"I require a little more data, Mrs. Phillimore," said Holmes, "Are any of your husband's clothes missing? Any personal effects, such as toiletries?"

"No, everything is just as he left it that morning."

"I see. May we have the address of Mr. Phillimore's law firm?"

"Of course. It is Killroy and Hay, 34 Austin Friars, EC."

"Thank you. And now, Mrs. Phillimore, we must bid you good day. Rest assured that your case has my entire attention.

"Now, Watson," said Holmes as we settled into a carriage on the Victoria-bound train from Bromley, "we can use the half-hour or so of travel we have before us to smoke a pipe or two and review the case of Mr. James Edward Phillimore. Let me have your thoughts."

"Well, your last question of Mrs. Phillimore tells against the idea that the whole thing was planned. Surely he would have taken some clothes with him if his aim was to leave her."

"No, I am afraid her answer doesn't prove that it was unplanned. He is a fairly wealthy man. He could, for example, have already rented himself a room somewhere, bought a fresh set of clothes, and established a new identity."

"Why did you ask the question, in that case?"

"Had she said, yes, there were clothes and toiletries missing, it would certainly have meant that it was planned. I was expecting a negative reply, but I had to ask. My belief is that his actions were a spontaneous response to something that must have happened to him in that brief span of moments. He saw something, or heard something, or possibly even felt something, that caused him to do what he did. But what?"

"Holmes! The deformed man in the street – that's what he saw! He must have known the fellow, and perhaps recognised him as someone who would use violence against him, and even against his wife. So he went back into the house and hid somewhere inside until his wife left for the police station. Then he came out and faced the man."

"Your idea has a certain amount of credibility, but there are too many points which contradict it. If Phillimore had genuinely forgotten his umbrella, then seeing the man was a strange coincidence. He suddenly had both a motive for going back into his house and an excuse for doing so. You may recall that Mrs. Phillimore described her husband as being the possessor of a strong physique, bookish and sedentary as he was. A man of the kind she described would be unlikely to attack someone stronger and fitter. And how do you explain the fact that the fellow ran away – or, as Mrs. Phillimore put it, hobbled away – when she looked at him? And yet, there is a possibility that in some way he is a factor. Perhaps it would be better if we waited to see if our visit to Killroy and Hay can shed any light on this. You have your newspaper, I see, and I my Pocket Library edition of Marcus Aurelius' *Meditations*, so let us spend the remainder of the journey reading quietly."

Charles Dickens would have found the premises of Killroy and Hay, Solicitors, familiar. The room filled with copyists and clerks, the smell of ink and wood polish and the rustle of documents, the self-important head clerk keeping a close eye on his young underlings, the short flight of stairs that led to the partners' rooms, the clients coming in and out, their faces beaming, sullen, or downcast, depending on the nature of their dealings with the law and how they had turned out – all were there. Holmes and I were shown into the office of Benedict Hay, a senior partner and a descendant of one of the founders of the firm, which I later learned dated back to the sixteenth century. Hay was a tall, thin man with wiry grey hair and piercing blue eyes. He shook us both firmly by the hand.

"Pray be seated, gentlemen," he said. "It isn't every day that our office is graced by the presence of so famous a visitor as you, Mr. Holmes. Oh, and you too, of course, Dr. Watson. I assume you are here because of the disappearance of our Mr. Phillimore. James is a first-class solicitor and we feel his absence deeply. His wife came here earlier today and said that she was about to consult you, as she had been disappointed in the response of the police."

"You last saw him this past Friday."

"That is correct, sir."

"In the last few days before his disappearance, was there any decline in the quality of his work?"

"None whatsoever."

"Was there any change in his general demeanour? Did he seem worried, for example, or overly excited?"

"No, he was the same as ever."

"Mrs. Phillimore told us that he sometimes worked late at the office. Would he have been here alone on those occasions?"

Hay's eyebrows lifted.

"Worked late? He never did that. None of the partners do, junior or senior. It is a policy of the firm."

Holmes briefly turned his head and met my gaze. I instantly understood the meaning of that swift glance. For the first time, we had caught Phillimore in a lie to his wife. There must surely be something he had been hiding from her. A double life, perhaps.

"Who is handling Mr. Phillimore's cases in his absence?" asked Holmes.

"That would be Mr. Ockendon, another of the junior partners."

"May we speak with him?"

"Certainly."

Hay took us down the corridor to another office. He opened the door without knocking and we found it occupied by a fresh-faced young man in his early thirties, who was in the middle of giving instructions to one of his clerks.

"This is Mr. Sherlock Holmes," said Hay, "and his colleague Dr. Watson."

The young clerk's mouth fell open, and he was clearly disappointed when Ockendon sent him off to carry out the work they had been discussing.

Hay departed for his own office.

"I take it you're here about Jim," said Ockendon.

"I believe there might be a key to his disappearance in the cases he was dealing with at the time," said Holmes.

"It's all fairly workaday stuff. A contested inheritance – that's *Jarrowby v. Markham*. Pursuance of a debt, *Laker v. Collins* – breach of promise. *Arlen v, Coniston* – an inquiry for the relatives of Michael Enderby. The – "

"Did you say – *Michael Enderby*?"

"Yes, sir. Michael Enderby. You'd have thought, being a lawyer himself, that Enderby would at least have left his papers in order when he died, but everything's in a terrible mess. He died intestate, and we're making inquiries to see if he had any relatives. I suspect he may not have been of sound mind at the end."

Holmes stood up and, reaching across the desk, shook Ockendon by the hand.

"Thank you, your assistance has been invaluable," he said.

"But I – "

I followed Holmes through the door, bidding Ockendon a polite farewell.

A minute or two later we were seated in a hansom bound for Baker Street. My friend was silent, a grim expression on his face.

"Don't keep me in suspense," I said. "You have solved the case, have you not? Or at any rate, are in receipt of a vital clue. What is the significance of this Enderby?"

"My friend, I advise you to wait until you are sitting in a comfortable chair in our rooms, with a strong drink in your hand, before you ask that question."

"Just as you wish."

"As a literary man," said Holmes when we were back in Baker Street, "and also as a lover of sensational fiction, you have no doubt read *The Strange Case of Dr. Jekyll and Mr. Hyde*, by Robert Louis Stevenson."

"I would hardly describe the work as sensational. Stevenson may have begun his career as a writer of boys' adventure stories, but he has a good deal of psychological insight. The business with the potion is somewhat far-fetched, but the work overall is a metaphor for the human condition."

"I stand corrected, my dear doctor. Clearly, then, you have read it."

"Yes."

Holmes poured us both a brandy, then reached into the coal scuttle and took a cigar from his box.

"It may surprise you to learn, then," he said, holding a match to the end of his *Hoyo*, "that while the work is fiction, it is based on fact. You recall the death of Dr. Anthony Adamson?"

"Yes, I read about it in an English newspaper, sometime after it happened, as I was in the base hospital in Peshawur at the time. He was a respected and highly-placed member of the profession, and only about fifty when he died. Of a heart attack, I think it was."

"Yes, that is what was given out at the time. In fact, Adamson is still alive, and incarcerated in an asylum. Stevenson based the character of Henry Jekyll upon him."

136

"You surely aren't suggesting that Dr. Adamson invented a potion that could transform a man both physically and mentally?"

"A complete physical transformation as described in the novel is, of course, impossible. But while, as you said, the potion is pure fantasy, it conceals a truth which can be scientifically verified, though it is far outside the experience of the majority of Englishmen."

"Holmes, you have yet to connect all this to Michael Enderby, let alone James Phillimore."

"This is what I believe has happened: Enderby was Adamson's lawyer, an old friend and the executor of his will, though he had no role in drafting it. Enderby died intestate, and the task of finding his relatives, as we heard this afternoon, was given to Phillimore, who then had access to Enderby's papers. Among them must have been either a summary of Adamson's own papers, or the papers themselves."

"Something in those papers is the key to Adamson's incarceration, and to Phillimore's disappearance."

"Just so. I shall keep you in suspense no longer, and I apologise if I have tried your patience. Over the years, I have made a special study of the effects of various types of hallucinogens. Oh, don't look so worried. My experience has been confined to reading up on them. As a medical man, perhaps you should look into them yourself."

"I hardly think that, as a general practitioner, I am likely to encounter their use."

"As I've said before, education never ends, and you never know when such knowledge may prove valuable. However, let us return to the matter in hand. One of the key aspects of such drugs is that they can cause a feeling of liberation, of transcendence. The Masatec Indians of Oaxaca in Mexico have for centuries chewed a hallucinogenic mushroom called *psilocybe* to achieve those effects. The ancient Greek worshippers of Dionysus appear to have used something similar. The Masatecs and the Maenads used them infrequently, mainly at religious rites, so their systems were able to recover from the effects. Repeated doses at short intervals, particularly if the taker is unused to them, can cause mania, and an absence of conscience which may be accompanied by bursts of great physical strength. Another symptom of frequent use is that the drug's effects may reoccur even if the individual hasn't used it for several days."

I was beginning, in a vague and tentative manner, to see where Holmes's argument was taking us, but I kept silent as he continued his narrative.

"I knew none of this when I was called in to help investigate the murder of Sir Daniel Cremers. I was lodging in Montague Street at the time, and living a more or less hand-to-mouth existence. Lestrade asked for my assistance, which I took as an admission that he had some small faith in me, though he wouldn't have said as much to a third person.

"There had been one witness to the crime, a maid servant, who had seen the murder clearly from her window. The night was cloudless and there was a full moon. She saw a white-haired old gentleman coming down the lane. The old man was accosted by a second man, whose face she couldn't see. He took out a bludgeon and without warning, in a burst of inhuman strength and rage, showered blow after blow on the head and shoulders of Cremers until the aged man fell dead to the cobbles."

"That exactly mirrors the murder of Sir Danvers Carew in the novel."

"Yes, but unlike the detectives in the book, we didn't have so straightforward a clue as the broken half of a cane belonging to the murderer. I had one very slender thread, which by great good fortune turned out to be a key to the mystery. From the maid's evidence that the killer had suddenly appeared, I conjectured that he had been waiting for Cremers in the house next to the maid's, which was derelict and untenanted. On the floor of that house, I found an old newspaper with a distinct bootmark upon it. As well as its size, there was a pattern on the rubber sole which suggested that it came from one particular bootmaker and had possibly been specially made. I might have saved myself much time and effort if I had told Lestrade and let his men do the legwork, but I preferred to do it myself. If I succeeded, I would get the credit, and if I had made a false assumption, only I would know of it. It was weary, uphill work, and had none of those features of interest with which you delight your readers. To cut a long story short, the boot led me to Dr. Anthony Adamson. I informed Lestrade, and Adamson was taken to Bow Street Police Station.

"He claimed to have no memory of the evening in question and could provide no one who could vouch for his whereabouts. In the cells later that day, he experienced one of those reoccurrences of the drugged state I referred to before. This involved some powerful hallucination, as he screamed loudly, claiming that all the other inmates of the holding cells had been transformed into semi-human monsters who were planning his death. An alienist who was brought into Bow Street to examine him concluded that this was a deep-seated mania and recommended that he be transferred immediately to an asylum.

"The alienist reported the situation to the British Medical Association, who then petitioned the Metropolitan Police Commissioner to keep the matter from the public in the interests of the dignity and reputation of the medical profession. Word was given out that Adamson had died of heart failure. He was given a new name in the asylum, and I was likewise sworn to secrecy."

"How did Stevenson find out about it?"

"A good question. One of the policemen or one of the doctors involved must have outlined the bare bones of the case to him, which he then covered with fictional flesh, producing that fable on the duality of man you praised a few minutes ago. Some years later, while I was investigating the effects of these substances, it occurred to me that some of the symptoms described exactly fitted Adamson. I gained permission to visit him in the asylum. He had accepted his responsibility for Cremers' death, but even after so long a period of abstinence from the drug he was still prone to those bouts of temporary mania. He confirmed that he had experimented with a cocktail of hallucinogens in an attempt, as he described it, to expand his consciousness beyond the confines and restraints imposed upon it by the strictures of society."

"But he became psychologically addicted, and continued to take the drugs even when the effect on him was deleterious."

"Indeed."

"I've seen other drugs have a similar effect. Opium, for example."

"So," asked Holmes, "are we now ready to apply our knowledge to the case of Mr. James Edward Phillimore?"

"I think so. Like Adamson, Phillimore longed for something beyond the bourgeois respectability of his life. Adamson's papers came into his hands, and he too saw a means of release in the use of these substances. Perhaps he was a little more cautious than Adamson, as Mr. Hay said that he could see no change in his demeanour or in his work. Phillimore may, as you suggested, have taken a room where he took small doses which had an effect, but didn't prevent him from going home to his wife the same night with his story of working late."

"Excellent, Watson! And what of his disappearance, the starting point of our labours?"

"No doubt you have reached a conclusion."

"Yes. Here is what I believe happened on that Saturday morning. As Phillimore and his wife prepared to leave the house, he began to feel the cumulative force of the effect of the drugs. He had, as you said, probably been taking them in small doses, but he had been doing so regularly. He must have felt that he was on the verge of some outbreak of madness, as he may well have been. He loved his wife and didn't wish her to see whatever it was that was about to happen to him. He deliberately left his umbrella behind so that he would have an excuse to go back into the house. He then made his exit through the back door, clambered over the wall and out into the street. That is when his wife saw him. He was the deformed man in the street."

"But you said there was no physical transformation."

"Not of the kind that Stevenson described, no. But one possible effect of these chemicals is muscular spasms, which can cause the victim to bend his back and lose full control of his limbs. He ran away as best he could to preserve his secret. Had Mrs. Phillimore been trained in my methods of observation, she might have noticed that the figure was clad in the clothes her husband had been wearing the last time she saw him."

"She did say that he was thirty yards away."

"True."

"This is all well and good, Holmes," I said, "but we are still left with the question: Where is James Phillimore? Is there any chance that he too has become a murderer? He must be apprehended, before, like Adamson, he commits some unspeakable outrage."

"Crimes of violence are common in the poorer parts of London, and the culprits seldom caught, so it is entirely possible that in the four days since he vanished, Phillimore has already committed some of those everyday atrocities which regularly go unsolved and unpunished."

James Phillimore was never seen again in this world, alive or dead, and his fate remains a mystery. Holmes was forced to swallow his pride and admit his failure, and his discomfort at being unable to provide any solace for the unfortunate Mrs. Viola Phillimore. Because this case is unsolved, and because of the unsettling nature of the revelations concerning Dr. Anthony Adamson's experiments, I am consigning this account to my old tin dispatch box in the vaults of Cox and Company, Charing Cross, where it will remain unread until seventy-five years after my death.

The Adventure of the
Unfortunate Cardinal

It was shortly before my friend Sherlock Holmes's retirement that we received the news that Pope Leo XIII had died. While neither Holmes nor I had any specific religious convictions, and the Pontiff's death hardly came as a surprise, as he was ninety-three years old and had been in poor health for some years, nevertheless, we heard the report of his passing with sadness. We had been of service to him on two separate occasions, the recovery of the Vatican cameos and the murder of Cardinal Tosca. While the first case received more publicity, Holmes was wont to dismiss it as "a little affair" because he had been able to solve it after a few hours' contemplation of the facts, without moving from his armchair. Needless to say, the Holy Father and his Cardinalate did not take the same view. The cameos dated back to the late fourth century and were said to have been created at the behest of St. Siricius, who had formulated many of the rules still adhered to by the priesthood. So, while they were not technically Holy Relics, they represented a link with the past whose absence would have been keenly felt.

As well as rewarding Holmes handsomely, Leo had been loud in his praise of the detective, and it cannot be doubted that this added to Holmes's growing international fame. Nor did it come as a surprise to us when, some years later, we were summoned to Rome to deal with the rather more delicate and potentially scandalous matter of the death of Cardinal Tosca.

The Cardinal had died, apparently from poisoning, not long after an unscheduled audience with the Pontiff. Holmes was uncomfortable if he had to leave his books and his scientific equipment, and the comforts of our life in Baker Street, for longer than a few days, so while the summons might have been expected, I was a little taken aback when he immediately dispatched a telegram agreeing to the trip. It transpired that, however complex or simple the case might prove to be, Holmes was eager to actually meet the Pope. I was happy to accompany him, for who could resist a journey to the Eternal City, even if the circumstances were unfortunate, and there was little likelihood that there would be time to view the full splendours of the ancient capital. Holmes informed Mrs. Hudson of our impending absence, and also sent a telegram to Inspector Lestrade to let him know that he would be unavailable for consultation until further notice. Then we were off, and we had ample opportunity to discuss the matter during the four days we spent on the Continental Express.

"What do you know of Cardinal Tosca?" Holmes asked me on the first evening after we had just finished a splendid meal and were partaking of brandy and cigars.

"Not very much, I'm afraid."

"Then let me enlighten you, as after we received the telegram I spent some time examining his career in my index, where I found him between a German music-hall performer and an

American admiral. The name is Italian, but he was French, born in a little village in Provence in 1857."

"Young to be a Cardinal."

"Indeed. His family was poor, but he managed, on the basis of his ability, to get a place at the Sorbonne. He apparently came to the priesthood after a long spiritual struggle, which I understand isn't uncommon among intellectuals who embrace the Church, but once in, his talent guaranteed him a swift rise up the echelons. There were those who thought he would be a worthy successor to Peter's chair, even though he would have been the first non-Italian Pope in four-hundred years – since Adrian VI, that is, who was Dutch. Leo looked favourably upon him at first, doubtless seeing in him a man of potentially equal ability to himself."

"I take it that something caused a rift between them."

"Yes, indeed. In 1891, Leo issued an encyclical called *Rerum Novarum* – in English, *Rights and Duties of Capital and Labour*. It was an open letter, passed to all Catholic patriarchs, primates, archbishops and bishops, and in it Leo rejected both socialism and *laissez-faire* capitalism, and championed the right of workers to form trade unions. Despite coming from a humble background, Tosca was opposed to trade unions. He believed that if employers operated their businesses on Christian principles, as was their duty, then there would be no need for unions, and in any case, they were the thin edge of a wedge that inevitably led to communism and atheism."

"And you think Tosca's death may somehow be connected to this disagreement?"

"Well, it is certainly a possibility, but it would be a capital mistake to assume that it were so until we have had the opportunity to examine all the data."

At the end of our journey, we were met at the elegant Stazione Termini in Rome by Cardinal Salvatore Lombino, a vigorous man with iron-grey hair in his early sixties who spoke near-perfect English, having spent some years in London as a young man as a deacon in St. George's Cathedral, Southwark. He was, duties permitting, to act as our interpreter throughout our stay. I had no Italian at all, and Holmes, characteristically, had little command of the language other than words connected with crime.

As a porter helped us load our luggage onto a smart little horse-drawn carriage, Lombino told us, "Accommodation has been arranged for you at the Hotel Emilio, which is in St. Peter's Square, within walking distance of the Apostolic Palace."

As it turned out, I would be glad of that last fact, for while that ride through the streets of Rome was a parade of magnificent buildings and places of historic interest, the surfaces of the roads were in bad need of refurbishment, which made for a jerky and uncomfortable journey, When we arrived at the Emilio, somewhat shaken up, Lombino gave us an hour or so to rest and refresh ourselves before taking us into the presence of the Pontiff. When we arrived at the Apostolic Palace, it transpired that unexpected business would delay the start of our audience, so Holmes took advantage of this waiting period to question Cardinal Lombino.

"Have you any idea why Tosca wanted to see the Pope?"

"That, of course, is a private matter between Cardinal Tosca and His Holiness, but it was clearly something urgent."

"Why do you think so?"

"Because a list is always prepared in advance of who the Pope will see and the order in which he will receive them. Tosca wasn't on the list. He simply arrived, sent in a note, and was admitted into the audience chamber on the Holy Father's order, before he saw anyone else."

"Do you have any idea why this was?"

"I can only speculate. Perhaps Tosca's faction had secretly grown, and he felt he had the power to urge the Pope to retract *Rerum Novarum*. But it seems equally possible that Tosca had come to assure His Holiness of his continuing loyalty, despite their disagreement and the growing number of his adherents. But – and this is the strange thing that seems to even further complicate the matter – there was another victim. He didn't die, but is seriously ill in hospital."

Holmes's eyes narrowed.

"Another victim? Who is he? Does he have any connection with Tosca, other than being high in the Church?"

"He is Michael Schwerzinger, the Bishop Emeritus of Sion in Switzerland. I think it doubtful that he and Tosca even knew each other, except perhaps by sight."

"Has Schwerzinger ever expressed any opinions about *Rerum Novarum*?"

"Not to my knowledge, no. In fact, Tosca was one of the few non-Italians who had strong feelings about it one way or the other. Nearly all his followers are Italian. Besides, my impression of Schwerzinger, from the little I know of him, is that he wants a quiet life in which he can enjoy the privileges of his position. I doubt that he would be drawn to factionalism of any kind."

"Has he been questioned?"

"No, the doctors have determined that at the present time he is too weak."

"Why was he visiting the Pope?"

"He isn't in Rome very often, so I imagine he was simply paying his respects."

"After we have seen Pope Leo, I would like to speak to the doctor who signed Tosca's death warrant."

"That is easily arranged. His name is Dr. Rizzio. Ah, I believe the Holy Father is ready for us."

To be in the simultaneous presence of Sherlock Holmes and Leo XIII was a remarkable experience. It need hardly be said that both were highly intellectual, but there was an immense contrast in the form that that intellect took in either man. It wasn't merely that the Pontiff was more than forty years older than the detective. Leo's faith had given him a serenity that underlay his sophisticated theological pronouncements. There was about him, above all, an impression that his very being was permeated with a sense of stillness.

In his most elevated moments, Holmes might attain a similar stillness – as when, for example, he was playing his beloved violin, or listening to a favourite piece of music. But his mercurial nature was such that this mood couldn't stay long in the ascendant. He might descend into near-despair when there was nothing of substance upon which he could exercise his formidable talents, or become voluble and excited when those same talents were being exercised to their highest degree, or, perhaps less forgivably, resort to sarcasm and mockery when dealing with the fumbling efforts of less-astute minds.

The Pope extended his hand for Holmes to kiss his ring but, despite the detective's respect for the Pontiff, he declined to do so, and I felt it incumbent upon me to follow suit.

Cardinal Lombino was horrified.

"You cannot insult the Holy Father in this manner!"

"We wish him no insult," said Holmes, "but we aren't of the faith."

When this was translated, the Pope looked severe, but nodded his head in deference to our principles.

"Let us continue," he said.

Having been given much of the information by Lombino, Holmes decided to keep the interview short in consideration of the Pontiff's advanced years.

"Do you still have the note given to you by Cardinal Tosca?"

"Yes."

"May we see it?"

"No, I am afraid not. Even though Tosca is with God now, the note, and our conversation, must remain confidential."

"Even though it might lead us to his murderer?"

"I assure you it would not."

"Then can you tell us what was said when Bishop Schwerzinger saw you?"

"It was simply a greeting, then an exchange about our health. Nothing more."

"One last thing: May we have the list of visitors for that day?"

"I will ask my secretary to make you a copy. The original must remain in the archives."

Lombino did not accompany us to see Dr. Rizzio in his office, as the doctor spoke excellent English, a legacy from a period at Barts in London.

Rizzio was a big man with grey hair and a neatly trimmed goatee. There was an air of professional expertise about him which inspired confidence. A brief conversation elicited the information that before he had been appointed the Pope's personal physician five years previously, he had worked in France and Spain, and, after he and his wife had decided to return to Italy to start a family, had done a fifteen-year stint as an examiner for the state police, followed by eight years in civil practice.

"I was called to the Hotel Emilio near St, Peter's – Do you know it? Visiting dignitaries are often lodged there."

"We are staying there."

"I see. Well, I often get called in if one of the Pontiff's guests falls ill, since they are mainly clerics of advanced years. When I arrived, Cardinal Tosca was in convulsions. My assessment was that these were caused by *Aqua Tofana*, probably in a highly concentrated form. Do you know of it?"

"A Sicilian poison," said Holmes, "odourless, tasteless, and colorless. First concocted in the seventeenth century and named after Giulia Tofana, who sold it to women who wanted to do away with their husbands."

"Quite so," said Rizzio. "I administered an antidote, but it was too late. The cardinal died twenty minutes after my arrival. He'd hardly passed away when I was summoned to the room of Bishop Schwerzinger, who was suffering the same symptoms, though not as severely. The antidote was successful, though he still needed to be hospitalised. I immediately asked the hotel staff if the two men had had the same breakfast, since if they had, there was the possibility that other guests might fall ill. But no, Tosca had had croissants and *cafe noir*, while Schwerzinger breakfasted on kipper with fried onions and oolong tea. I sent a message to the Holy Father's secretary to inform him of the situation, and was told not to bring the matter to the attention of the state police."

"Thank you, Dr. Rizzio."

We later dressed for dinner, then went down to the ground floor to the Emilioo's restaurant. But before we went in to dine, Holmes approached the reception desk and asked for the room number of Monsignor Noonan, the second name on the list given us by the Pope's secretary.

"He's in room 127," said the receptionist, in heavily-accented but near-perfect English, "but he's at table eighteen in the restaurant if you want to speak to him now."

The monsignor was a short, stocky Irish-American with a head of wispy greying hair. His nose and ears bore signs that he had boxed in his far-off youth. There was an aperitif glass before him, half-drained, so he must have been waiting to be served his meal.

"Monsignor Noonan?"

"That's me. Whom have I the pleasure of addressing?"

His accent could only be from New York.

"I am Sherlock Holmes, and this is my colleague, Dr. Watson."

"The detective? Then I guess you're here to investigate the death of poor Tosca."

"Yes. Did you know him?"

"A little. Can't say I agreed with him on everything. *Rerum Novarum* struck me as exactly the right stance for the Church to be taking. Still, Tosca was an upright sort of man, and I don't think anyone questioned his right to follow the dictates of his own conscience."

"May I ask you," said Holmes, "were you ill on the morning of the fourteenth?"

Noonan made an amused face at the oddness of the question, then said good-naturedly, "Well, since you ask, I was a little nauseous, and a bit dizzy, but I lay down for about half-an-hour, and then I was fine. How did you know?"

A waiter was approaching Noonan's table with a tray bearing a bowl of soup, a plate of vermicelli, and a glass of wine.

"I didn't. I was testing a theory. Thank you for corroborating it. And now we shall leave you to enjoy your meal in peace."

"Have you come to any conclusions?" I asked Holmes as we climbed the hotel stairs after finishing our own meals.

"Well, I think I know how it was done, but as to who, and why? That will take a little more investigation."

We had arrived at the adjacent doors to our rooms. I said, "It seems to me that all we have is that what the three have in common is that they all had an audience with the Pope. And for some reason, however the poison was administered, it was done in decreasing doses."

"What else did all three do in the audience chamber, besides talk to the Pope?"

I thought for a few seconds.

"Presumably they all sat down."

"True, but that wasn't it."

With that enigmatic statement, he entered his room and closed the door.

The following morning we stood once more before the Pope, but this time the role of translator was taken by the Papal Secretary, Lombino being occupied on some other business.

"Thank you for seeing us again," said Holmes. "We have only a few questions. First, does anyone have access to your bedroom at night, other than yourself?"

"Only my head of security, Mateo Bisch, and his deputy."

"Which one was on duty on the night in question?"

"Bisch."

"Would he have access to the following day's audience list?"

"Of course."

"Your Holiness, are you a heavy sleeper?"

"What is the possible relevance of such a question?" the Papal secretary demanded.

"It is relevant, I promise you. Please translate."

The Pope replied with a wry smile.

"Yes, I am. The burdens of office . . . ."

"And lastly, do you remove the Papal ring when you go to bed?"

"Always. When I am awake, I am Leo XIII, Pontifex Maximus, Head of the Roman Church, Christ's Vicar on Earth. In my nightshirt, without the ring, I am once more, for a few brief hours, only Gioacchino Pecci from Lazio."

"And you keep the ring by your bedside?"

"Yes."

"Thank you. And now, Sir Secretary, if you can arrange it, we will need a small room in which we can question Mateo Bisch, with a member of the Swiss Guard posted at the door."

Mateo Bisch was a tall, muscular man in his late thirties with a strong-jawed but sensitive face below close-cropped dark hair.

"Signor Bisch," Holmes began, "it is a tenet of your faith that confession is good for the soul, so I give you this opportunity to tell us freely how and why you brought about the death of Cardinal Tosca."

Bisch put his elbows on the table in front of him and said nothing.

"Very well, I shall tell you the how. You went into the Papal bedchamber once you were sure the Pope was asleep and you smeared his ring with concentrated *Aqua Tofana*. You did this because you knew that the first thing that happens in a Papal audience is that the visitor kisses the Pope's ring. Even that little contact would be enough to kill. But you overdid it. You killed the first man, but enough remained on the ring to make the next man gravely ill, and even then there was enough left to make a third person dizzy and nauseous. And then of course there is the fact that you killed the wrong man. Your target wasn't Cardinal Tosca. It was Bishop Michael Schwerzinger. You saw the list of audiences the previous evening and realised that at last your opportunity had come. You couldn't know that Tosca would arrive early the following morning and see the Pope before Schwerzinger. Am I right?"

Bisch's features writhed.

"Oh yes, you are right, you oh-so-clever Englishman, Mr. Sherlock Holmes."

"Why do you hate Schwerzinger enough to want to kill him?" I asked.

Bisch stood up.

"You ask me why? Why? I'll tell you why! Because he is a foul, disgusting creature! Because he killed my brother, as surely as if he had put a bullet through his head. I had to make my own justice. Where was justice for Alesio, if I didn't make it? I swear, I would go into that hospital and squeeze the life out of him now with my bare hands if I could."

Bisch fell back in his chair, put his head into his hands, and burst into passionate sobbing.

Holmes and I fell silent. At length, Bisch wiped the tears from his face with the back of one large hand.

"All my life, I have been a devout son of the Church. All I ever wanted was to serve it in some capacity. I wasn't academic enough, or unworldly enough, to join the priesthood, but I was tall and strong and vigorous, so I applied to join the Swiss Guard, and was accepted. When I was deemed too old for the Guard, I sought a job in the Vatican security service, and again was accepted, and rose to be the chief.

"I was born in Basle of a good family, the oldest of eight children. We have all served our church or our country with honour – all save one. Alesio, the youngest. He started out well. Better than I, certainly. He was a good scholar and sang in the church choir, but then, around thirteen or fourteen, he started committing petty crimes. He went to drink and cocaine, and joined a gang of ruffians. His crimes became more serious, and eventually he was sent to prison. I believe the shame of it hastened my parents' deaths. I was now the head of the family, and as such, it was my duty to visit him in that terrible place.

"I could scarcely believe that the piece of human wreckage I saw before me was my own flesh and blood.

"I was bitterly angry with him. 'How did you come to this'? I yelled at him. 'How could you sully the family name? You were a better scholar than me! You were a choirboy . . . .'"

"Tears rolled down his cheeks. 'Yes, a choirboy,' he said. 'That's where it began.' I asked him what he meant, and he told me a horrible story. If I hadn't been there – if I had not seen the sorrow in his eyes, and heard the pain in his voice, perhaps I would not have believed him. He had loved his choirmaster like a second father, and when the man singled him out, he believed that he loved him like a son. But then the choirmaster began . . . *interfering* with him. He forced him to commit obscene acts. Alesio felt that this was wrong, but the choirmaster was an adult, and a respected priest of the Church. Who could he tell? Who would believe him? Was it his fault? Had he invited it without knowing? What would his life be? These thoughts rolled around and around his head until all he wanted was escape from the pain they caused. Alcohol and cocaine numbed him. They also led him to crime. I thought that telling me of his pain might exorcise it.

Instead, it brought it closer to the surface. He suffered. A week later he took his own life.

"The choirmaster left Basle. He had friends high up in the Church who helped him rise. You know his name, and what he became. Now do you see?"

"I see that if your brother told the truth, Schwerzinger was guilty of a heinous crime. Why did you not report it?" asked Holmes.

"I could not prove it! Who would believe me? Who would even consider it possible? Now I have caused the death of an innocent man, a good man, even if he had his disagreements with the Holy Father. For that I must die."

* * * * *

"Well," said Cardinal Lombino, "the killer wasn't a priest. That's a relief. No scandal on that score. Now he has confessed, it will not be necessary to inform His Holiness of what Bisch claims was his motivation."

"Perhaps not," said Holmes, "but you might do well to investigate any other claims against Schwerzinger."

"Well, that is something for the Swiss Police. Now, the Pope is very appreciative. He would like you to stay another week, as the Church's guests. I'm sure you would like to see the Sistine Chapel, the Castel Sant Angelo, and the rest of the marvels of the Eternal City."

Holmes and I exchanged glances.

"Convey our greatest respects to the Pontiff, but I think we have had enough of Rome for the time being," said Holmes. "Perhaps you would arrange for a carriage to take us from the Emilio to the Stazione Termini."

Shortly after our return to Baker Street, Holmes received a telegram from Cardinal Lombino informing him that due to a severe reaction to one of the curative drugs that had been prescribed to him, Bishop Michael Schwerzinger had died in hospital of a massive heart attack.

I hadn't even considered the idea of turning our experiences in Italy into one of my accounts of my doings with Holmes, but the death of Leo XIII brought it back to my mind. It was a sordid tale, and yet, Holmes's intellect and deductive powers were well on display. I record it here, and will place this narrative in my old tin dispatch box, with instructions that it be published something past seventy-five years after my death.

The Disappearance of the
Cutter *Alicia*

One morning in June 1926, I was pleased to find, among my meagre correspondence, a letter postmarked from Sussex. I knew of only one person living in that particular county, and instantly recognized Holmes's handwriting, which, though he was a mere two years my junior, was as firm and clear as it had ever been in those far-off days when we had shared rooms together. I confess that I felt a thrill of the old excitement as I eagerly slit the envelope open.

My dear Doctor,

I trust that you are in good health. You may wonder at my writing to you after so long a silence, but the enclosed papers, which are in the nature of a death-bed confession, finally provide the solution to a long-standing mystery. You went so far, in the introduction to one of your little fables, as to describe our participation in the case as "a complete failure". But now I find that my speculations, wild as they may have seemed at the time, had some basis in truth, though of course they went unsubstantiated. I refer to the affair of the cutter Alicia, *which sailed into a patch of mist and disappeared, and whose crew were never heard of again.*

The sting of Holmes's few defeats had remained in my memory just as clearly as the elation of his many successes, and I laid the letter on the table and fell into a reverie.

That year saw Holmes at perhaps the peak of his powers and the greatest height of his international fame. The social status of any potential client was entirely irrelevant to him, and while he was far from indifferent to the state of his bank balance, he refused to examine many cases which would have brought him a princely fee in favour of those which offered him an intellectual challenge or appealed to his sense of justice.

It was, I recall, a fine morning in late spring. Holmes was looking through a pile of the letters and telegrams which were now arriving at our lodgings every morning. I confined myself to a close examination of the morning papers, for I knew that if he found nothing in the post to pique his interest, his next move would be to ask me if there was anything worth scrutinizing in the news.

"Well, well, " he said suddenly, "it seems that wonders will never cease."

He waved the thin paper of a telegram in my general direction.

"We are about to have a visitation from my brother, Mycroft. Now, as you will recall, he rarely leaves the fixed circle of his existence to visit these humble rooms unless it is to warn us away from a sensitive subject, or to engage our assistance with something he perceives as being of national importance."

"Well," I said, lowering the newspaper, "you must admit that he has been generally right about the latter. So which is it?"

I smiled as Holmes read out the telegram in a fair facsimile of his brother's somewhat deeper and more portentous tones.

"*'Sherlock – Drop whatever case in which you may be involved and expect me to call on you at eleven o'clock this morning on a matter of national security. Be sure to be in your rooms at that hour. Mycroft.'*"

Holmes tossed the telegram onto his desk and rubbed his bony hands together.

"To do him justice, every case he has brought to my attention has been of interest. Luckily, he calls when I have nothing on hand. You will recall that I sent a message to Gregson at Scotland Yard last night."

"Yes."

"It was the final piece of evidence that will secure the prosecution of Thomas Lansdown. And as for the Treharne matter, I am confident that there will be no new developments in the next few days. Was there anything in the papers that might be connected to Mycroft?"

"Not that I saw."

"Then perhaps the matter is still secret."

"We'll soon find out," I said, pulling my watch from my waistcoat pocket. "It's almost eleven now, and your brother has never been less than punctual."

Holmes rose, went over to the window, and gazed down into the street.

"His carriage is just arriving now, and he isn't on his own."

"Lestrade? Bradstreet?"

"No, I've never seen the man before."

There was a knock at the downstairs door, and shortly after we heard the heavy clump of Mycroft Holmes's ascent, accompanied by the sound of the footfalls of a somewhat lighter man.

The older Holmes brother entered, accompanied by a shorter man whom I took to be in his early fifties. His wavy brown hair and beard were sprinkled with grey, and his face was somewhat swarthy and creased with lines. He was wearing a black pea-jacket, dark canvas trousers, and a pair of heavy brown boots.

"This is my brother Sherlock, and this, his friend and colleague Dr. John Watson," Mycroft Holmes began, "and this, gentlemen, is Arthur Coppard, the – "

"Indulge me, Mycroft. Let me exercise such small powers as I possess."

"Oh, if you must."

Holmes took Coppard's hand and shook it vigorously.

"I am pleased to meet you, Mr. Coppard. You are a sea captain, though you have come up through the ranks from a private seaman, and haven't been in your present position for very long."

"That is true, sir, but how did you know it?" Coppard said, in an accent which smacked of the West Country.

"Mycroft, would you care to explain?"

"No doubt my brother observed you leaving my carriage and coming with me to the door. Though a short distance, it was enough for him to see that you have that distinctive gait which is the mark of one who has been long at sea. When you entered the room, he noted your air of authority, which indicated your position of command, but when he shook your hand he felt its hardness, and the callouses which come from the work with ropes and tackle which is the lot of the common seaman. Hence, you haven't long left the fo'c's'le for the captain's cabin."

"Well," said Coppard, "I hadn't thought there was one such a man in the world, let alone two!"

"Let us be seated, gentlemen," said Holmes, " and you can tell us the reason for your visit."

Mycroft gestured to Coppard that he should speak.

"I am Arthur Coppard, captain of the *Christabel*, a ship in the employment of the Liverpool Cotton Association. We transport raw cotton from the Americas. A week ago, we were making our way back to the port with a full cargo when I saw a cutter some five-hundred yards to the west of us. Apart from the fact that she was a little far out to sea for such a small vessel, she appeared to be in distress, for she was moving erratically, with the changes of wind and current. There seemed to be no one at the tiller. We shifted our course to go to her aid and, as we did so, she entered a patch of mist. We followed, but when the mist dissipated a few minutes later, the cutter had vanished. Into thin air, not a sign of her."

"Had the mist entirely dissipated when you noticed the cutter's disappearance?" asked Holmes.

"No, there was some left a few feet above the water, but it was clear that the ship had somehow vanished, so we turned our course to Liverpool, and I told the authorities what I had seen at the earliest opportunity."

"Thank you, Captain Coppard," said the elder Holmes. "I must ask you now to return to the carriage and await me there, for what I must now discuss with my brother is a case of national importance."

"As you wish, sir. Good day, gentlemen."

"Do you wish me to leave too?" I stood up as the sailor made his way downstairs.

"Stay where you are, Watson, " said Holmes. "My brother knows that it is both or neither where you and I are concerned."

Mycroft raised one broad, flat hand in a gesture of acquiescence.

"So, Sherlock," he said, "what do you know about smuggling?"

"I assume from Captain Coppard's story that you are referring to smuggling by sea, rather than across land borders. When I embarked on my examination of the various forms of criminality in this world, I studied the subject with some assiduity, but I confess that since fewer cases involving smuggling have come my way, my knowledge of it has somewhat atrophied. I'm aware that it still exists on the western coast of the United States, in China, and some parts of Africa. It used to be widely practised in the West Country, but surely that ceased at the beginning of this century."

"Well," said Mycroft, "not entirely. It still occurs from time to time in that part of the country, and all the coasts of the British Isles are still regularly patrolled to prevent it. That brings us to the relevance of Captain Coppard's experience. The majority of the boats performing that service are cutters. The only such vessel that hasn't returned to its designated berth is the *Alicia*, currently captained by one Albert Hutchinson. My suspicion is that the craft Coppard saw was the *Alicia*, and the reason that she was moving erratically, why there seemed to be no one at the tiller, was that the crew had been abducted. Now, if that is the case, our national safety is at risk."

"How so?" I asked.

Mycroft answered, slightly impatiently. "Of necessity, all the captains of the cutters employed by the government in this capacity are kept informed of all the movements of all the craft plying the coast, and this includes those patrolling the sea against the possible incursion of foreign vessels whose intent is, shall we say, not peaceful. If Captain Hutchinson has fallen into enemy hands, they may force him to reveal what he knows, enabling them to evade the security patrols and attack the mainland. Now, thus far we have had no such events, but the situation must be resolved. Captain Coppard and his crew have been ordered on pain of prosecution to keep silent about the matter. Now, Sherlock, I am leaving this in your hands because I have more immediate business to deal with. A revolution in San Bartolo is imminent, which threatens our mineral interests in that country, and there is the possibility that the Korean *won* will be subject to inflation. Good day, gentlemen. Should you wish to contact me, you know where I am."

"A pretty mystery, is it not, Watson? And in his understandable eagerness to ensure the country's safety, Mycroft ignored the chief feature of the story: How did the *Alicia* vanish after sailing into that patch of mist, whether its crew was on board or not? It is a mystery which by its nature might seem to most who hear the story to be explicable only in supernatural terms. Was the *Alicia* the victim of some giant, undiscovered creature from the sea bottom which rose from the depths and dragged the cutter and its unfortunate crew down to destruction in a matter of moments? Or perhaps Captain Hutchinson was a sinner equal to the legendary Vanderdecken, and the Devil rendered the ship invisible and sentenced him and his crew to sail the seas until Judgement Day. Or if, like the mathematician Charles Howard Hinton, we wish to dress our speculations in a cloak of pseudo-science, then the ship may, in some inexplicable manner, have entered another dimension. There is, of course, a more simple and fully rational explanation."

"Which is?"

"You studied Latin and Roman history at your school, I imagine?"

"Yes, of course."

"Then you will no doubt remember that the notoriously debauched Emperor Nero was also a matricide."

"Yes, and when the assassins came for his mother, she pointed at her womb and said, "Strike me here," because it had been guilty of bearing such an unfilial son."

"Correct. But before that he tried another method."

"How is any of this connected to the fate of the *Alicia*?"

"Patience, my dear Doctor, patience."

He stood, went over to his bookshelves, and took down three volumes, opening each one after another and skimming through the pages until he found the passages for which he was searching.

"Here is Suetonius, from his *Twelve Caesars*," he said," passing me one of them. I read:

> *Nero's next stratagem was to construct a ship which could be easily shivered, in hopes of destroying her either by drowning, or by the deck above her cabin crushing her in its fall.*

"And Tacitus, from *The Annals*."

> *The vessel had not gone far, Agrippina having with her two of her intimate attendants, one of whom, Crepereius Gallus, stood near the helm, while Acerronia, reclining at Agrippina's feet as she reposed herself, spoke joyfully of her son's repentance and of the recovery of the mother's influence, when at*

a given signal the ceiling of the place, which was loaded with a quantity of lead, fell in, and Crepereius was crushed and instantly killed.

"And lastly, Cassius Dio's *Roman History*."

Sabina, on hearing about this, began to persuade Nero to get rid of his mother in order to forestall her alleged plots against him. One day they saw in the theatre a ship that automatically separated in two, let out some beasts, and came together again so as to be once more seaworthy, and they at once had another one built like it.

"Now, Watson, I am sure you will concede that if there were shipbuilders in the First Century who were capable of constructing such a vessel, it would present no problems to a modern builder who would have access to our century's superior techniques."

"The accounts don't exactly agree."

"True, although they all concur that Agrippina survived by swimming to shore. Suetonius is often accused of purveying malicious gossip, and while Tacitus has a somewhat better reputation, he is not without his critics. Dio was writing a little later, but still, most of our contemporary historians think the story essentially true. I think we can take the use of such a stratagem as a working hypothesis in the case of the *Alicia*. You may have noted that I asked the good captain if the mist had entirely dispersed. If he hadn't turned the *Christabel* and left before it was completely gone, I fancy he would have seen wreckage floating on the water. The presence of both the *Christabel* and the mist cannot have been planned, so the perpetrators presumably intended flotsam bearing the *Alicia*'s name to be found."

"But why was it done? And by whom?"

"Clearly, what our friend the captain saw wasn't the *Alicia* herself, but a collapsible replica, as I don't think it would be possible to alter an existing vessel to fall apart in that manner. This implies that the real *Alicia* is still in existence somewhere, and that there are those who gain an advantage from her being believed lost."

A thought suddenly occurred to me.

"Holmes! Supposing the *Alicia* has been captured by smugglers. In her, they might approach other Navy boats, which, perceiving her as friendly, would allow her to draw alongside. The smugglers could then swarm aboard and kill or capture the revenue men."

"That isn't impossible, but such a theory has an insurmountable flaw: If it had happened, would Mycroft not have informed us? He can be secretive, true, but he would gain nothing by concealing the fact."

"Who, then?"

"The only others who could carry it out would seem to be the crew themselves. They would be able to take her into a harbour where it could be duplicated. It must have been a long-term plan, since the construction of the false *Alicia* would take some time. I have no experience of such matters, so I don't know how long, but it must surely be measured in weeks."

"But why should they do such a thing? What advantage could they gain from it?"

"It would be believed that they were dead, drowned in the sinking of the vessel. To me that hints at some crime in which they were all complicit. Dead men are notoriously difficult to prosecute. Now, unless it can be proved that all combined to carry out some crime on land, which I consider unlikely, we must consider those crimes which are connected with the sea."

"Mutiny?"

"As I said before, the construction of the false *Alicia* must have taken some time, and mutiny is usually carried out spontaneously, or at least planned not long before the act. I am inclined to think that, as with so many misdeeds in this fallen world, monetary gain is at the heart of it. Who could they steal from with absolute impunity? The smugglers themselves. Let us say that they captured a smuggling vessel which had accumulated a large amount of loot. Tempted by greed, they take the money and dispose of the smuggling vessel's crew. But how are they to spend the money without arousing suspicion? Presumably there is enough, cutters' crews being small in number, for them to start new lives elsewhere, so they secrete the money in a safe place, using some of it to pay an unscrupulous shipbuilder to construct the false *Alicia*. They then sail away in the real one, after setting the replica adrift at sea. Will it serve?

"I'm sure you have hit on it. But there are problems."

"Indeed. How do we prove it, and even if we can, how do we bring the perpetrators to justice?"

I will not try the reader's patience with a lengthy description of the fruitless efforts we made over the ensuing weeks. The wives and families of the missing men were interviewed by Mycroft's agents, but they clearly knew nothing of the matter, and were given financial help on the basis that their menfolk appeared to have died while in the service of the government. The only shipbuilder with criminal antecedents who could be identified had left the country, which supported but didn't corroborate Holmes's hypothesis. In the end, he was forced to concede defeat. Mycroft Holmes was far from satisfied with this outcome, but his annoyance with his younger brother subsided when none of the dire predictions he had made that morning came true.

And there it had stood for many years. I turned my attention once more to Holmes's letter.

> *I received this communication from a gentleman in Australia who signs himself* P.J. Webb, *although from the internal evidence, assuming the tale is true and not some peculiar hoax, he would seem to be in truth Arthur Swinscomb, the youngest of the six crewmen of*

the Alicia. *In any event, I am sure it will be of interest*
to you, as it was to me.

Yours sincerely,
Sherlock Holmes

The enclosure read:

Dear Mr. Holmes,

    My doctor informs me that I have little time left
in this world, and before I depart it altogether I would
like to make my confession. I have never been a
religious man, and have no conception of what, if
anything, awaits me when I have quit this life. Word
reached me that you were charged with the
investigation into the disappearance of the cutter
Alicia.

[Next to this was a marginal note in Holmes's handwriting:
This suggests that despite Mycroft's precautions, Captain
Coppard revealed that he had visited us, though how that
information then reached Swinscomb is likely to remain a
mystery.]

    I would gain no solace from conversation with a
priest, but as I know you came to no firm conclusion

concerning its fate, [No doubt he had read that piece of sensational fiction you entitled "The Problem of Thor Bridge"!] *it would please me to finally enlighten you after the passage of so many years. I believe I am the last survivor of our little band of brothers, and so there is none other who can perform this service, and I now have no family to be adversely affected by my revelation. I was the youngest of us, but I was, nevertheless, a grown man, in full control of my destiny, so I cannot use my relative youth as mitigation for my misdeeds.*

I was born in Whimple, in Devon, to honest God-fearing parents, and I swear it is no reflection on them that I turned out the way I did. I was as proud as a man might be when, at the age of twenty-three, I was assigned to the cutter Alicia, *with the responsibility of keeping a section of the west coast of our islands free from smugglers. In truth, we rarely encountered any, but we proudly put that down to our presence, and felt sure that had we not been there, the sea would have been rife with them. There were six of us, including the captain, Albert Hutchinson. He was a tall, imposing man with a great red beard. He was hard as nails and brooked no nonsense, but he was generous and fair, and we all respected him.*

His mate, Thomas Groome, had served with him for several years, and when he was assigned to the

Alicia, *it was only natural that Groome should join him. Groome was almost as tall as Hutchinson, but was slim and wiry, and could scramble up the rigging with the speed and surety of a monkey. Next came John Tremayne, at forty-seven the oldest of us all, fair-haired and golden-bearded, still fit and muscular though probably not fated to stay in the service for much longer. Then there was Simon Gascoyne, who had come from what was known as "a good family", but had joined the Navy after that family had been bankrupted by bad investments. A few years my senior, he too was taller than average, with a face that remained pale no matter how hard it was battered by the weather, slim with curling dark hair.*

Bob Roberson, my closest friend on the Alicia, *was, like me, of middling height, though we didn't resemble each other in any other respect. He was married and I was single. He was fair and I was dark. He was loud in his laughter while I was quiet and shy. He loved to gamble, drink and sing, while I kept a close hold on my money. But of all my comrades, he was perhaps the easiest to like.*

We all worked together as a smooth unit under Captain Hutchinson's steady eye and there were no complaints of our conduct by those in charge. What, then, caused our downfall? What led to one of us lying dead on the deck of the Alicia *and the others dispersed to the corners of the world?*

In a word, greed. The oldest trap in the world. The love of lifeless pieces of paper and metal that somehow becomes more powerful than the sense of duty and responsibility towards one's fellow-man. And in truth, though the money we took has assured me a comfortable life, it has also been a lonely one, with the shadow of my guilt hanging ever over me.

Enough. To my tale. If you were a man of the sea, and especially if you were also a native of the West Country, you would have heard of the legend of Black Bart's Treasure. Of all the smugglers of the eighteenth century, he had been the most successful, and the story was that he had secreted a vast hoard somewhere, in some cave on the Devon coast. His plan was to make one final smuggling voyage and then escape with his accumulated wealth to the New World, but on that last voyage he had quarrelled with his first mate and in the course of a bloody duel with cutlasses, each killed the other. A storm then hit the ship, and it went down to Davy Jones' Locker. One sailor escaped, clinging to a piece of wreckage, and after he was found on the shore he survived long enough to tell the story to his rescuers. So the legend grew up, and in time it was said that there was a curse on Black Bart's loot. Perhaps there was.

Like Black Bart's ship, the Alicia *was caught in a fearful storm. The night was falling fast, and there was no sign of a lighthouse. But unlike Black Bart, in the teeth of a storm we managed to make our way to safety in the form of a sheltered cove. We dropped anchor and prepared to spend the night, but there was no fresh water on board. Bob Roberson and I volunteered to go ashore and look for some. What we found, instead, was a cave. With typical bravado, Bob suggested that we go inside and look around, for who knew, maybe Black Bart's treasure was in there.*

And yes, against all reason, and in keeping with a hoary, improbable tale, that was what we found. Some of it was in the form of paper money unusable in this day, but the majority of it was gold and silver coins, innumerable great piles of them. Like the two honest fellows we felt ourselves to be, we went back and told the others of our find. Soon all six of us were there, staring at more money than we could have hoped to see in a dozen lives. It was then that the great sickness of greed began to overtake us. I certainly knew in my heart that this wasn't ours, that we should notify the authorities to come and retrieve it, that such an injection of money would greatly benefit the county and even perhaps the country. Were we not bound to be given some reward, some honour, for the selfless act of handing it over? No doubt this went through all of our minds, but not one of us said anything to that effect.

We began instead to discuss how we might escape with it, how it could alter our lives so much for the better. Those of us who were married, Groome, Tremayne, and Roberson talked of how they couldn't bring any of it home to their wives and families without arousing suspicion. It was Groome who said that if we could make it seem that we had perished at sea, then our families would get compensation and we could take the hoard aboard the Alicia, *drop anchor on a foreign coast and divide it. Then we could scuttle the ship and go our separate ways. From there the plan grew with the relentlessness of an avalanche. Gascoyne knew of a boat builder who could make a replica of the* Alicia. *When, just before our next scheduled voyage, we consulted him, he assured us that if nails made of beeswax were substituted for certain crucial iron nails, it would be possible for the ship to drift on the ocean until the heat of the sun and the action of the seawater melted them, at which point the false* Alicia *would collapse into wreckage. With luck, that wreckage would eventually be found and our loss confirmed.*

The weeks during which we awaited the replica's completion were tense. None of us were able to speak of it, but then one day John Tremayne found his voice.

All six of us were on deck when he said, "I can't keep my peace any longer. What we are doing is wrong. You know what I'm saying. Abandoning our families, all for gold and silver. Betraying the trust that's been placed in us. Dammit, in your hearts you all know it isn't right!"

"So what would you have us do, Johnny?" asked the captain. "Go back to our lives of toil and danger when there's a way out, a way to safety and a comfortable life? Is that what you want?"

"All right. If I can't move you, at least I can go."

"Then go," said Gascoyne, "and more for the five of us."

"How do we know you'll not betray us? asked Groome.

"We don't," said Gascoyne.

Suddenly there was a flash of smoke and the report of a gun, and to my horror I realised that Bob Roberson had shot Tremayne, who fell to the deck with a scream of pain. Moments later he was dead.

"That solves the problem," said Bob, and I stood aghast at the transformation of my best friend into a cold-blooded killer. In that moment, I knew that I was complicit, that as a participant in the whole scheme I shared in the guilt of Tremayne's death.

"Don't look so pale, boy," the captain said to me. "Help me throw his body overboard."

The rest you can no doubt deduce. Everything went according to plan. Where the others went, I cannot say. I used my share to carry myself to the other side of the world, as far as I could from England.

Signed this day, the 18th May, 1926, by

P.J. Webb

Acknowledgements

Thanks must go first to David Marcum, editor of the MX Sherlock Holmes series, for his help and encouragement, which helped me extract more from Watson's tin dispatch box than I would have thought possible, and to Steve Emecz, publisher of the series.

Then to my friends both in the UK and the Czech Republic who have had kind words for my stories, both Holmesian and otherwise: Eva Zahradnickova, Jana Kubesova, Frantisek Holik, Martin Plant, Petra Pachlova, Alan Gray, Tomas Dubeda, Misa Cankova, and (in NZ) Ramsey Margolis. And lastly, to the late Michael Ballard, a good writer and a good friend.

MX Publishing

MX Publishing brings the best in new Sherlock Holmes novels, biographies, graphic novels and short story collections every month. With over 500 books it's the largest catalogue of new Sherlock Holmes books in the world.

We have over one hundred and fifty Holmes authors. The majority of our authors write new Holmes fiction - in all genres from very traditional pastiches through to modern novels, fantasy, crossover, children's books and humour.

In Holmes biography we have award winning historians including Alistair Duncan. Brian Pugh and Maureen Whittaker who have all won the Sherlock Holmes Book of The Year Award.

MX Publishing also has one of the largest communities of Holmes fans on Facebook and Twitter under @mxpublishing.

MX is a social enterprise that has raised over $130,000 for good causes including Happy Life Mission (Kenya), Undershaw School for children with learning disabilities (UK) and the WFP (World Food Programme).

www.ingramcontent.com/pod-product-compliance
Lightning Source LLC
Chambersburg PA
CBHW070025260626
47159CB00005B/1954